GETTING IT BACK

Tristram Felix

ISBN: 978-1-4457-5755-1

For those who really understood

'Such was that happy garden-state,

While man walk'd there without a mate.'

(Andrew Marvell 1621-1678)

CONTENTS

1

Dazed

The shops were still there. They looked the same, but he didn't really see them. It was the first Saturday morning after his world had ended. He walked slowly and deliberately along the pavement, occasionally brushing past the shoppers who were intent on their needs. They didn't really notice him or his staring, blank eyes, nor he them. He hadn't shaved for six days; he'd hardly washed in that time either, other than for one particular public appearance. He was sweating, even though it was a cold March day — the consequence of a solitary drinking session the previous evening in a quiet pub four miles out of the village in the neighbouring town of Fliston, followed by a curry from the *Taj Mahal*, consumed at one that morning. The taxi driver had had to help him into and out of the cab — and carry the take-away to his front door. His mouth was dry and he could still taste the Lamb Bhuna. He was hung-over and tired — very tired, and it was more than physical tiredness that was numbing his senses. He was tired of his new situation even though it had only been — he peered at his watch — six days, eleven hours and seventeen minutes. His mathematical brain still worked, then.

Market Camton was a large village, as villages go; it had everything that was needed for a commuter watering hole situated forty miles north and west of England's second city. One main street, lined with shops, contained everything necessary for the residents. Several side streets contained everything necessary for visitors — antique and gift shops and the like. The village had a supermarket but it was hidden from view of passing motorists, being located down one very narrow lane that led to a concrete open space that once formed the car park of the defunct railway station. Even the advertising sign had been placed discreetly high above the pavement. Andrew Grey turned into Pig Lane and headed for the anonymity and bright lights of this supermarket. He hardly noticed the gentle touch of a hand on his right shoulder. The voice was familiar, if a little nervous.

"Andy, it's good to see you, mate. How have you been?"

Andrew didn't really slow his pace; both because the words had hardly registered in his mind and because he didn't really want to talk to anyone — not yet, not ever, maybe. He wanted a quick shop in Tescos and home to the safety of his home — their home. The hand became wrapped round his shoulders; he was almost being manhandled, and he didn't like it. Sweat was dripping off his brow. He didn't look to his right as he angrily shrugged his shoulders.

"Get off, you…."

The man released his grip that had been offered in a comforting way.

"Oh, sorry, mate. I just wanted to make sure you were alright."

Andrew stopped walking and tried to focus his blood-shot eyes on the cause of his anger.

"Oh, it's you, Kev. I didn't see you there."

Kevin Simpson smiled warmly. His large hand returned to massage Andrew's back.

"You know Sally and I are here for you, mate, don't you?"

Andrew had now turned fully to face his friend and colleague of ten year's standing.

"Yeah, I know, Kev. I just need time on my own — I'm not really ready for any social contact yet. Sorry."

"That's OK; I'll let you get on your way. You…."

Andrew Grey turned quickly away before his friend had a chance to finish the inevitable sentence that would have surely been a comment on his dirty and dishevelled appearance. Though Kevin Simpson would never actually utter them, Andrew could hear the words echoing in his head,

'*You look awful, mate.*'

He didn't look back, and Kevin would report back to Andrew's colleagues on Monday at Castlemount Grammar School — the school where they both taught and from which Andrew had been granted two weeks leave of absence. In fact, it would amount to a break of four weeks, owing to the impending Easter break. Andrew Grey would need every minute of those weeks — and many years more.

He felt more comfortable as he entered the modest-sized supermarket. He just had to avoid any of his pupils. Fortunately, with Castlemount Grammar situated twelve miles from Market Camton in the neighbouring town of Camton Magna, such a meeting very rarely occurred. Though it was past eleven, the aisles were surprisingly empty of shoppers. Many of Market Camton's residents had objected to the building of the year-old supermarket and still insisted on making their everyday purchases in the High Street. It was too early in the season for the village to be inundated with visitors from Birmingham and further afield, drawn there by its picturesque setting in the wooded and hilly countryside above the Shropshire dales.

He wasted no time — he knew what he wanted — two six-packs of strong lager and a bottle of his favourite Irish whiskey. His stomach was still churning with nervousness and apprehension at his appearance in public. He'd better get some food. Grabbing some frozen ready meals and a large wedge of cheese, hardly glancing at the variety, he turned his trolley round and made quickly for a vacant check-out. He hesitated; sweat breaking out on his forehead again. The check-out was being 'manned' by an ex-pupil of his — Mary Jones. He backed away up an aisle, on the pretext of grabbing a loaf of bread and, making a detour down another aisle, he headed for a second check-out, almost out of sight of the first. Had she seen him? Why did it bother him? What was he afraid of? She had been one of his better-behaved students and he'd always liked her. He just didn't want to be confronted by anyone that knew him. That was it. He had to get out into the crisp spring sunshine. There was now a queue of two at his selected check-out. He'd had enough. He couldn't stand it anymore. His head was throbbing from the excesses of the previous evening and he abandoned his trolley to run blindly for the exit, almost tripping over some boxes, as he did so. Mary spotted him. She called out,

"Sir? Are you alright?"

He didn't turn round nor halt his panicky run until he had turned into the relative dimness of Pig Lane. He was breathing heavily. His overweight forty-one-year-old body was out of condition, the result of not enough exercise over the previous eighteen dark months. He hadn't looked after himself while he had been.... He shuddered and leant against a shop frontage. Eyes peered out and stared at him. He started to run again. He had to get out of the village — anywhere would do. He made up his mind — he would drive into the dales and find a nice, quiet country pub where nobody knew him. He would drink himself into oblivion and let fate determine his future. He didn't care that he was still well over the drink-drive limit. His life meant nothing now anyway. His modest cottage was just off the High Street on the other side to Pig Lane, less than five minutes from where he was. He idled to a stroll — better not to draw any more attention to himself. He was quite well-known in

Market Camton. The sun was bright now as he crossed the High Street. His tired eyes squinted. He thought he heard his name being called. Head down, he made it quickly into Church Lane. *Rose Cottage* was about a hundred yards past St Clements Parish Church. It had been a mild winter and the front lawn needed mowing. The garden in general was in a sorry state — its care had not been a priority for many months. He was half-way up the flagstone front path before he noticed the matronly figure peering through the letterbox. The woman turned sharply and sheepishly on hearing Andrew's footsteps.

"Oh, Andy, I'm glad you're here. I thought you must be still out. Kev said he'd seen you in the village. I've made a couple of pies for you — one meat and one apple. I thought you could use some home-cooking. I've been meaning to bring them round since Thursday, but …."

Sally Simpson paused as Andrew approached. She tried to hide her shock at her husband's best friend's appearance.

"Are you alright, Andrew, love?"

"I'm fine, Sal."

'*I just want to be left alone*,' he thought, but added instead,

"I'm just on my way back out to see some friends from school — just been to do some shopping."

Sally glanced at Andrew's empty hands and whether it was this apparently confident lie or the sight of his awful appearance, Sally took the hint and nervously handed him the carrier bag. She stood on her tiptoes and gave him a quick peck on the cheek, whispering,

"You take care now, Andy, and remember we're right here if you need us. We'll look after you, don't you worry."

With that Sally Simpson patted Andrew's arm and hurried past him out into Church Lane. The Simpson's cottage was another two hundred yards down the lane — it was now too close, thought Andrew and he didn't want anyone looking after him — there was only one person he wanted to do that for him. The tears came again — floods of them — so many he could barely see to put his key in the lock. He flung the carrier bag onto the kitchen floor. He heard a plate shatter. He picked up the keys to the Focus from their place on the hook behind the kitchen door and within a minute he was backing the silver Ford down the stony track that was adjacent to the cottage — the track that led down to the woods at the back of the cottage. The woods where he and ….

The CD player was on very loud as he drove, drowning out his thoughts.

'*Four who want to stone me,*
Two who want to own me,
One says she's a friend of mine.
Take it easy, take it easy.'

He turned the volume down a little. The words started him thinking again. He didn't have any friends — he'd only had one friend — Rachel, and she had left him. She was his friend. She was the only friend he wanted. Not Sally; not Kevin; not the others; not his brother, Tony; not his parents — not anybody. The good part of his life was dead. Yes, he'd been angry over the last year or so. Ever since the diagnosis of the brain tumour, he'd been angry. Angry at God and angry at himself, because deep down he felt it had been his fault. It had been the previous Saturday evening when she had finally succumbed to the ravages of the disease and he knew she was now at peace. He was not. He'd been plagued all week with feelings of guilt. He kept telling himself that there was nothing he could have done, but he couldn't rid himself of the nightmare. If only he hadn't met her, married her and taken her away from her parents' home town near

Norwich. He had disturbed some kind of equilibrium — he just knew it. He had as good as killed her himself. He recalled Rachel's mother's words on their wedding day: '*Now you look after her, Andrew, or you'll have me to answer to.*' He recalled the look on Dorothy Bateman's face when he said he'd got the teaching job in Shropshire. The Bateman's had been bakers in Middleton for nearly a hundred years and, at twenty, their daughter Rachel played a major part in running the business. It had been all she had known all her life, from well before she had left the local high school at sixteen. He should have stayed at Middleton High, even though the prospects of promotion had looked thin. He would have made Head of Maths eventually. Old man Cooper had only six or seven years to go, but Andrew couldn't wait that long and when the post came up at Castlemount, the young couple got married in haste — mainly for Rachel's parents' sake — they had insisted the wedding had to be in Middleton. That had been July nearly seventeen years ago and he had just turned twenty-five. He would be one of the youngest Heads of Maths anywhere, particularly in a grammar school. He had been teaching for three years. The tears started to roll down his face again as the guilt of his naked ambition came back to haunt him for the umpteenth time. He had to get off the A458 — he could barely see to drive through the tears. He spotted a sign ahead and he could hardly believe his eyes. It had to be an omen — some kind of comforting reminder of a previous life. The sign read *Ripley 2 miles*. He even managed a wry smile. *Ripley* had been the name of his pet dog when he had been a boy growing up in Canford on the East Anglian coast. Without bothering to check in his rear-view mirror, he braked hard and just managed to swing the car left into the narrow country road.

His mood seemed to lift as he reached the village, and *The Dog and Pheasant* was easy to find, facing the village green. Even the dog painted on the overhead sign looked a little like his pet mongrel. It would only now need Rachel to be sitting at the bar and he would believe that he had died somewhere on the road and gone to heaven. There was one space left in the small car park and, as he steered the Focus into it, he was overcome with a strange feeling of anticipation, even though he knew he wasn't going to see Rachel.

Turning the engine off, he glanced in the rear-view mirror and, probably for the first time, he was struck by his appearance. He *did* look awful. He took out his hairbrush and attempted to put his fair locks into some kind of order. He reassured himself that the stubble looked almost of the modern designer kind. Blowing into his hands, he also convinced himself that his breath was a little sweeter than it had been so far that morning. Opening the driver's door, he took a sharp intake of the cold, country air and exhaled noisily. Somewhere a clock sounded the hour — it was one o'clock.

The small country inn was surprisingly busy for such an out-of-the-way place. A mixture of serious walkers and more social ramblers filled the small main bar with muddy boots and anoraks — the conversation seemed to centre on the technicalities of the best local routes in the dales. Andrew made immediately for the one vacant spot in the only reasonably quiet corner. He climbed onto the stool and ordered a pint of the local brew — of considerably less strength than he had been used to that week. He had to take it steady if he was to last for any length of time in his chosen watering hole, and he needed to try to sober up a little to consider his present situation.

"Here for the walking, sir?"

The voice came from the landlord who had just served him, and Andrew suddenly realised that his appearance probably stood him apart from the rest of his host's clientele. He tried to answer in his normal teacher's voice.

"No, just out for a drive and stopped for some refreshment."

"You won't have too much, sir, will you…?"

The ginger-headed portly landlord paused and continued,

"… if you're going to continue to drive, I mean — only the police have been targeting one or two pubs in the area, especially at weekends."

"Thanks for the advice, but I just want a *quiet* drink, mate."

The landlord grinned — he'd understood the new customer's meaning and he walked away to strike up a conversation with some regulars. Andrew took a long swig of his ale and smiled — he began to relax, particularly as he'd seen the '*rooms available*' sign hanging above the bar. Though he hadn't really wanted to chat with the landlord, he was beginning to feel the need for human contact — just so long as that contact was with people who did not know him. Kevin, Sally and his other friends would probably not understand how he felt but that was just too bad, as he suddenly recalled what the vicar who had presided over his wife's funeral had said:

'*Remember, Andrew, be good to yourself — you are the most important person now.*'

He drank slowly; he forced a cheese ploughman's down. He wanted to think deeply about the tragic change in his circumstances. Rachel's funeral at St Clement's had been arranged quickly and already it seemed a blur to Andrew, even though it had only taken place on the Thursday afternoon. Her parents had returned to Norfolk late on Friday — they could see both from their son-in-law's appearance and from his demeanour that he wanted to be left on his own. He had been grateful for their insight and also for Kevin and Sally's help in arranging a quick burial. It had been an effort for Andrew to maintain some kind of dignity given the four previous days of solitary drinking. Indeed, if it had not been for Rachel's father, Arthur, chaperoning Andrew on the eve of the funeral, he might well not have made it in an upright state. The Batemans had arrived around teatime on the Wednesday and Arthur had insisted on taking Andrew to *The Royal Oak* that evening. Andrew had seemed reluctant to go with his father-in-law and actually managed to continue the pretence for a couple of drinks. Both men shed a few tears later that night, once Arthur had eventually persuaded Andrew to stumble home just before closing time.

He missed his brother. Tony Grey lived in New Zealand with his wife and three children, and they had not made the funeral. Andrew just wished they could have been there. As he ordered his third pint — the local bitter was to his liking and he didn't feel the need to change to something stronger — he began to think on his and Rachel's lack of children. They had tried, and tried, but to no avail — there hadn't seemed to be any medical reason for their infertility — it was just one of those things, their doctor said. In the end, they had resigned themselves to a life without children. It had had its advantages, socially and financially, but ….

The pub was emptying. The walkers and ramblers were off for their afternoon exercise in the dales. Andrew glanced at his watch — it was twenty past two. Only a small crowd of drinkers remained, gathered in front of the widescreen television for the Wales versus England rugby match. As Andrew climbed off his stool to join them, a sobering thought occurred to him. If he and Rachel had had a family, he would not be in his present self-indulgent position. They would have been his priority now — not himself. He would have had to have been strong for them. He sighed; he didn't have any children and he couldn't change that — or invent the crutch of a family. He sighed deeply; he would wallow in self-indulgence awhile yet. He had done enough thinking for the time being — now for some social contact. He was here to enjoy himself. Feelings of guilt could wait until later. He knew those feelings would haunt him forever but right now he was going to be *good to himself.*

It was clear that among the dozen or so men and one woman, whose physical appearance suggested that she played the game herself, there was a sprinkling from the principality. Andrew quickly joined in the conversation.

"When's the game start, mate?"

"Five minutes — and get ready for a thrashing, my friend."

The lilting tones marked the man down as one of the opposition.

"You're a long way from home."

"Not really, it's less than fifty miles to God's country, you know."

Andrew smiled. How far had he driven? The man seemed friendly enough.

"Are you local?"

"Market Camton."

"Quite a way from here, boy — been walking?"

"Something like that."

God Save The Queen had finished. The teams were lined up. Further conversation would be rugby orientated for the next forty minutes.

"Buy you a pint, mate?" asked Andrew.

"Thanks, I'll have a Guinness — can't stand English beer. The name's Owen by the way."

"I'm Andy."

Andrew drained his glass and headed for the bar. His social contact was going well. Though the Welsh were not his favourite people, at least he had a drinking buddy. He was in a round and he felt comfortable.

Another couple of pints and his assimilation into a larger round formed by Owen and his two compatriots began to relax Andrew still further. Even the half-time score of 18–15 to the enemy could not dampen his lifted spirits. The necessary call of nature, entailing a longish walk, to the gents at the rear of the pub was accomplished with some bumps to his thighs — he would discover some bruises later that would puzzle him as to their explanation. His unsteadiness did not go unnoticed by mine host and he made a note to challenge the stranger if and when he decided to leave. Owen was in triumphant mood on Andrew's return.

"So you were going to win the championship, eh?"

"Hooky's playing a blinder," added one of his friends, Phil.

"Yeah, what a try," said Owen.

"We'll come back, mate," said Andrew.

"Yeah, but you won't get enough points to catch France, old boy."

"Juss as long as we beat you, frien'."

Owen winked at his friends. The Englishmen was already slurring his words. They would have some fun.

With England only scoring a penalty in the second half, the Welsh eventually ran out fairly comfortable victors by 27 points to 18. Long before the final whistle, Andrew had taken up a sedentary position in a threadbare armchair, both for his own safety and that of the other watchers. He barely heard the singing of '*Hymns and Arias*' that had started a few minutes before the end. Only Owen and his two friends had remained to see James Hook complete the remarkable feat of scoring at least one of each of a try, conversion, penalty and drop goal. The quick transformation from relative soberness to sleepy-eyed drunkenness had been aided by the double whiskies that Owen and his cronies had added to Andrew's pint glass, both on their individual rounds and surreptitiously at other times when his gaze had been averted. They left him to his slumbers and made their way out into the late afternoon sunshine, intent on some solid sustenance at the other inn in Ripley where they would continue their celebrations long into the evening.

The landlord did not disturb his sleeping customer and was content to leave him to recover somewhat. Andrew's car keys were carefully removed from his jeans pocket and hidden away behind the bar. Before returning to engage conversation with the only other drinkers left — a couple of regulars — mine host alerted his wife upstairs to prepare a room for the stranger.

2
Amazed

He needed some bread that Saturday morning. He'd moved into his rented flat the day before and he only had coffee, milk and sugar. He was due to start at Middleton High on the Monday — his first teaching post after his PGCE and Maths degree from the University of East Anglia. He was just twenty-three, but with his blond good looks and slim frame, he could still pass for a mature teenager. Middleton was a quiet country town, not unlike Canford where he had grown up, except for the High school which drew pupils from a wide radius in the Norfolk countryside. Though Canford was much smaller, and only classed as a village, the general ambience of Middleton had made Andrew feel at home from the day he had got the teaching post back in May.

Though it was only just after nine, the sun was warm — the forecast was for another hot day. August had been wet and Andrew was glad that the weather had recently changed for the better and was set fair for a nice weekend before he started his career in earnest. A relaxing stroll through Middleton's shopping area was what was needed — to get his bearings. He would probably take a walk past the school as well to see how long it would take on foot. He seemed to recall it was on the western edge of the town past the municipal cemetery. His flat was towards the eastern boundary — the top floor of an Edwardian terrace, one among half a dozen similar properties in a quiet residential street.

As he strolled towards Middleton High, he made a mental note of the traditional looking bakers, right in the heart of the town; Bateman's by name. They had some tasty looking filled rolls in the window. A couple for his lunch would not go amiss and some hot toast for his belated breakfast. On arrival outside the school, he felt a little disappointment — on the day of his interview, he hadn't noticed the graffiti and general run-down nature of the buildings. Had he looked at the school through rose-coloured spectacles when he'd been offered the post? Oh well, he thought, mustn't judge a book by its cover. Let's enjoy the weekend and not worry about his decision. However, he *would* worry, though. He'd always been a worrier, a trait inherited, no doubt, from his mother. It had stood him in good stead academically — three A's at A-level and a first class degree in Mathematics. Even research had been a possibility, but his tutors sensed it might be a struggle and had advised against it. It probably '*wasn't his métier*'. He noted that the main gates seemed to be open but he quickly decided against further investigations of his new place of work and turned back for the town. It had taken him exactly twenty-five minutes — he would try to get into the habit of walking most mornings, weather and books permitting. In any case, his rusting Mini wasn't the best starter in the morning and he'd kept his bicycle as back up.

Bateman's was busy when he arrived — always a good sign, he thought. The young girl behind the counter caught his attention immediately and he couldn't help but stare. While he waited in line, he noticed that she glanced his way on more than one occasion. He felt decidedly hot under the collar. He was lacking completely in experience of the opposite sex — his studies and general shyness had prevented him from striking up any kind of relationship so far —he would realise much later in life that this was something else inherited from his mother. Though he was tall and strikingly handsome, he felt inadequate and embarrassed by his body. Even taking showers at school had been an ordeal for him. He was beginning to perspire freely.

"Yes, sir, what can I get you?"

The accent was broad Norfolk. He stammered his reply.

"A l-large loaf, please."

"What kind, sir?"

"Oh, er, wholemeal."

"The girl turned to the shelves. Andrew noticed the shape of her body through the loose-fitting dress and apron.

"Would you like it slicing?"

"Er, yes please, that's very kind of you."

He was more confident now. She smiled sweetly.

"No problem, sir, that's five pence extra. One pound exactly."

He handed over the coin. Her hand seemed to linger longer than was necessary as he took the bread.

"Thanks," he said. "See you again."

The girl smiled again. This time it seemed more than just a smile born out of natural courtesy. He took the loaf and turned quickly away. It wasn't until he had gone a hundred yards or so that he realised that he'd forgotten any rolls. He could not go back — it would be too obvious, and definitely too forward?

His first day at Middleton High went well — the pupils seemed to be somewhat in awe of him. Had his academic profile preceded him, or was it his honeymoon period? As he sauntered back to his flat, he felt good. His timetable looked excellent — two top sets in years 10 and 11 and the rest was sixth form teaching. They were using his mathematical ability to the full. Even the prospect of an afternoon of junior games and some year 12 General Studies didn't dampen his spirits. He was confident he could cope, and as he entered Middleton's main precinct, his thought turned to exercising that confidence in another area. He would get some bread from the bakers.

"Yes, sir, w-what can I get for you?"

This time, the girl seemed nervous. Andrew looked at her and held his gaze for a few seconds.

"Oh, hello again, I'll have the same as before."

"Which was, sir?"

She feigned ignorance. Her heart was beating faster. She hadn't forgotten the slim, handsome stranger, who looked little older than her.

"A large wholemeal, please."

His heart was beating faster, too. Dare he ask her the question that he'd never asked another girl in his life?

"Slicing?"

"Y-yes, please," he stammered. It was now or never.

She turned away to the machine. She seemed to bend provocatively over it.

"Would you …?"

She turned back to him. The machine hummed in the background.

"Yes, sir?"

"Would, would you put in a bag, please?"

She gave him an odd look and then stifled a laugh.

"Of course I will — I doubt you could carry it home in bits, sir!"

Andrew blushed deeply. He handed over a pound in silence. He hadn't done it. He didn't notice the slight disappointment in the girl's face. She tried to help him in his indecision.

"You're new in town, aren't you?"

There didn't seem to be anyone else in the shop.

"Yes," he replied, his confidence returning. "I've just started at the High School today."

"What — you're a teacher?" she asked with some surprise.

"Yes – Maths."

“God, you must be bright. I’ve got a good head for figures — my dad always made sure of that — I’ve been helping in the shop since I was ten, but I couldn’t fathom Algebra and Trig.”

Andrew relaxed a little.

“My name’s Andrew, by the way.”

“Nice to meet you, Andrew.”

Still the right words wouldn’t come. He turned away and just reached the door.

“See you again, Andrew — I hope,” she called out.

He turned back and smiled.

“Hope so too, er …?”

“Rachel, it’s Rachel Bateman.”

“Hope so too, Rachel.”

And with that, he was gone. He didn’t want her to look long on his deep red face. It had been a new experience for him — it hadn’t been flirting as such but it had been a conversation — and with the baker’s daughter, he thought. For her part, Rachel was unusually cheerful that evening. Her parents would exchange knowing glances — they had seen that look on their daughter’s face a couple of years previously. They hoped this one wouldn’t end in disappointment.

Andrew did not next call at *Bateman’s* until Saturday — he had not wanted to appear too keen, and he had resisted the temptation to buy a packed lunch each day. For one lunchtime duty a week, he received a free meal each day. His sense of anticipation was soon quashed when he realised that the baker’s daughter seemed to have alternate Saturdays off. He did not dare enquire of her father where she had gone, but a chance decision, that he would later regard as providential, led him to drive into Norwich, twelve miles distant. He needed some shirts and a couple of pairs of decent trousers for school and he had made no plans for the day, other than his original intention. He was now at a loose end so it seemed a good idea.

He spent a good couple of hours in the city and was just making his way back to the multi-storey car park when he heard his name being called.

"Andrew?"

The voice was familiar and his heart skipped a beat. Clutching his M & S bags, he turned abruptly to see Rachel Bateman waving at him from the other side of the road. She was alone and pre-empted his attempt to cross over the busy road, skipping nimbly between the traffic. Andrew's jaw could not fail but drop, albeit metaphorically. Her auburn hair flowed like waves in the breeze — she'd had it under a white cap when he'd seen her on the previous occasions. She was at his side in a moment, her hand lightly tapping his bare forearm — almost the first physical contact he'd ever experienced with a member of the opposite sex.

"Hi ya — I thought it was you. What are you doing in Norwich?"

Though his plastic carrier bags said it all, he knew it had been a nervous attempt at some kind of ice-breaking. He grinned broadly.

"Shopping?"

"Me too, but I didn't buy anything. I just had a coffee with an old school friend and she had to go home early."

She was gabbling nervously, but she had also joined him at his side as they walked together. Andrew could not believe what was happening to him. He had to take control of the situation, but what were you supposed to do? He made a stab in the dark.

"I'm just on my way back to Middleton. Would you like a lift, Rachel?"

Even saying her name out loud had been difficult; particularly after the several dreams he had had that past week. None had started like this, but this would do.

"Are you sure you've finished all your shopping?"

"Yes, I'm all done. My car's just in the multi-storey near the castle."

"Then, yes please, Andrew — the bus to Middleton is only every two hours on a Saturday and the next one's not till four."

Andrew glanced up at a clock. It was two-thirty. They walked the half mile in virtual silence. He felt uncomfortable in female company. He could smell her perfume and occasionally their arms brushed. Once, even her hair briefly clipped his face. Once back at his car, he felt more at ease. He had to be in control now. He was going to drive Rachel back to Middleton and he no longer felt nervous. He took charge of the situation. Trying to act the perfect gentleman, he escorted her to the passenger door and made a faux bow as he opened it.

"Your carriage awaits, my lady."

"Thank you, kind sir."

He soon joined her and together they set off back to their quiet rural town, both somewhat relieved after the hustle and bustle of the large city. After nearly ten minutes negotiating the one-way system, while Rachel remained quiet to allow her new friend to concentrate, they eventually reached the open road. They both tried to speak simultaneously. Andrew quickly gave way.

"Sorry, you go first."

"I was going to ask how your first week had gone."

"It went well — the kids seem nice."

"They are, to begin with, but they'll also be checking you out. We used to do it to any new teacher. Let them relax and let them think they've got us under perfect control for about the first two weeks, then …."

"Then?"

"Then one or two friendly tricks."

"Friendly?"

"Yeah, friendly — you know, designed to embarrass you a bit. I'll let you into a bit of a secret."

"What?"

"The name game."

"And what's that?"

"Well, how many of each group you teach can you honestly say you know the names of yet?"

"About a third, maybe."

"Well, in about another week or so you'll probably know the majority, right?"

"I would hope so."

"Well that's when they'll play the name game."

"You still haven't told me what it is."

"It's easy. When you talk to a pupil by name, albeit quite correctly, they'll say, '*I'm not John, sir, or I'm not Tina, sir, that's …*' and they'll point to someone else. Three of four conversations like that in a lesson and you'll doubt yourself as to whether you've got any of their names correct."

"Hmm, I see," replied Andrew thoughtfully. "And how do I win this game?"

"You don't — just play along with them. They need to know that you're on their side and can take a joke. Join in and deliberately start calling some of them by the wrong name. Old man Carpenter started calling some of the boys by strange names like Isaiah and Mephistopheles or in one case by a girl's name. He's about the best liked teacher there. They'll see the funny side and realise you like them. Whatever you do, don't get angry and shout. They'll know they've got you then and other less savoury pranks will follow. All kids want to be liked by their teachers. Then they'll trust you and do anything for you."

"Quite the little child psychologist, aren't you?"

"Not really, just five year's experience at Middleton High. It's a fantastic school and the vast majority of the kids are friendly and want to work, once …."

"Once they know you care about them."

They were on the outskirts of Middleton and were about to pass the school. Andrew had learnt as much about teaching children in ten minutes as he had in a term at university.

"Drop you at the shop, Rachel?"

"No — by the record shop will do. You know where I mean?"

"Yes," he replied quietly. He suspected she wasn't quite ready to show her parents how she had got back from Norwich. He drove the final few hundred yards in silence — neither really knowing how to continue their chat as they neared the inevitable parting of the ways. In the end, when the car had stopped, Rachel just lightly patted his knee and jumped out of the car with a,

"Thanks, Andrew, see you later."

She was gone before he could reply — or ask the question he'd been planning in his mind from the very moment he'd set eyes on her. He felt frustrated and he made up his mind there and then that the next time he saw her he would definitely ask *that* question. For the time being, he had to cope with some early marking and a few hours' preparation for his second week, so his mind would be sensibly occupied. As a priority, on Monday morning, during his one free period, he would study as many files of the pupils he taught as he could, paying particular attention to their photographs and making appropriate notes as he did so. If he only got through his Year Eleven, it would at least be a start.

It had to be Monday on the way home from school. He could wait no longer. He would just come right out and ask his question — and no pretext of buying bread this time. Surely she had encouraged him. Though he was totally lacking in experience in such matters, he knew he could not miss this opportunity. He made several mistakes in his teaching that day — so obvious, even the weakest students had sniggered a little. He was the first member of staff out of the gates at the end of school and five minutes later, he arrived breathless outside the bakers. She was there and being late afternoon the shop was devoid of customers. As he strolled nonchalantly in, he hoped her father was not around. She seemed to be expecting him.

"Hi, Andrew, what can I …?"

"Rachel," he interrupted.

"Yes?"

Her smile was inviting.

"W-would you like to go for a drink sometime?"

"When?"

"Er, next Saturday evening?"

"Yes, I would love to?"

Andrew seemed stunned — amazement written all over his face. A girl had said yes — he had a date with a member of the opposite sex! Her smile was warm and she continued,

"Where are you going to take me?"

"Oh, maybe somewhere out of Middleton — a quiet country pub."

"Good idea, Andrew — perhaps it's not sensible to go to one in town."

Andrew thought he understood. Middleton was a small town and tongues might wag — not good, given his position or Rachel's popularity amongst her customers.

"Are you going to buy something, sir?"

The gruff voice seemed to come out of thin air. Rachel half turned and hid her reddening face from him. Her father had started to emerge from the shadows at the back of the shop.

"*I said: are you going to buy another drink, sir?*"

The second voice was different and more distant than the first. Andrew's head suddenly seemed heavy. The voice became louder.

"*Best you stay the night, sir, I think. You can't drive in your condition.*"

Then he was awake — and he understood. It had all been a dream — but it had been so real, even down to remembered words and phrases. Had it all started like that? He seemed to have recalled so many things that he had forgotten over the last eighteen years. His neck ached and his head was swimming. Now he felt really awful.

"I'll make you a strong black coffee — on the house, sir."

He pulled himself up in the chair and groaned from his sore neck and back.

"Just a glass of water, please," he managed.

"The wife has made a room ready for you. I've put your car keys on a side table there. Do you want anything to eat?"

He tried to stand to feel in his pocket for his missing keys. How had they been taken? He sighed with resignation and promptly fell back into the chair.

"Easy, sir. I'll help you upstairs before the evening rush starts."

“Wha-what’s the time?”

“It’s just gone six, sir. You’ve been asleep for well over the hour. Feel any better?”

Andrew mumbled incoherently and groaned again. The landlord helped him stand. Thoughts and blood rushed through his head. It had been *so* real — had it really only been and hour or two?

The cold water on his fragile stomach was to cause him to bring back much of what was left there. He peed long and with great relief. He slept without dreaming that evening, waking only once to visit the toilet again. The landlord’s wife checked on him a couple of times — the last occasion being just after closing time. He was snoring loudly and he would not really come to until dawn the following morning. On wakening, he struggled hard to recall his dreams, without success — just a vague memory of a sweet young eighteen-year-old girl who had once amazed him by saying ‘yes’.

3

A New Kind of Freedom

It took all of Sunday and much of Monday for Andrew to recover from his 'ordeal'. He steeled himself to avoid alcohol at all costs — he hadn't yet really considered his new position without the stimulant in his blood stream. By the time it got dark on Monday, yes, he felt tired, but he was definitely sober. Apart from a brief phone call from New Zealand on Sunday evening — his brother was just off to work on their Monday morning — he'd had no other human contact, for which he was relieved. He hadn't even spoken to the landlord of *The Dog and Pheasant* on the Sunday morning — he had left as soon as it had got light, both to avoid any embarrassing questions and to get back to the safety of *Rose Cottage*. He had hoped that the fifty pounds he left on the bar together with a brief thank-you note would be sufficient recompense for the landlord's time and trouble. He'd left his telephone number just in case. Fortunately, it had been relatively easy to let himself out — no awkward alarm system to deal with.

As he sat down in front of the television just before seven-thirty that Monday, he suddenly realised that he hadn't tried to relax in this way on any of the nights since that awful Saturday nine days previously. *Coronation Street*, one of Rachel's favourite programmes, was about to start. Out of years of habit, and without being asked, he turned the channel over to ITV. Then something new hit him. He'd never really liked the 'soap' — in fact, truth be told, he hated all 'soaps'. He didn't need to watch it anymore. Suddenly, he felt guilty — Rachel was going to miss it. Should he watch it for her? Surely he should. This was stupid, he thought, I can watch what I like, can't I? He hit the teletext button on the remote control and checked the evening's schedule. There was a documentary on financial 'scams' on BBC2. He changed channels again. He was free to watch what he liked. It had been years since he'd had that responsibility or independence. But wait, he had no right to enjoy himself, had he? Oh, this was intolerable. How stupid was he being? Then the tears started to roll down his cheeks again. How on earth was he going to cope when he went back to Castlemount Grammar in three weeks time? He turned the TV off and got up to brew a cup of tea — something to do to take his mind off the decision that he just failed to come to terms with. The phone rang. He hesitated before taking the receiver off its cradle on the kitchen wall. How ought he to sound? Cheerful? Sad? He tried to speak normally.

"Er, hello, Andy Grey speaking."

There was a pause before Kevin's voice said,

"Hello, mate, just ringing to see if everything's O.K. Didn't see your car in its usual place in the track on Saturday evening."

"Er, no, I went for a drive, Kev. Clear my head, you know."

"Must have been a bloody long drive, mate. It wasn't there even at eleven."

Oh, why couldn't people leave him alone? He didn't have to explain his movements, surely, did he? Kevin wasn't his keeper.

He said nothing, hoping that his friend would move on to something else.

"Anyway, mate, Sally was wondering if you'd like to come to dinner one night this week, maybe Thursday? We could go to the pub afterwards — like we always used to before …."

"Oh, I don't know, Kevin."

"It would do you good, Andy — get you out and about again. It must have been hard while you were looking after Rachel."

"Maybe, Kev — let me think about. I'm not really ready for socialising just yet."

He managed half a grin, as he remembered Saturday's over-indulgence in social activity. He just wished he could tell his friends, yes, and his family, that it was easier, much easier to talk to complete strangers than to them.

"O.K., Andy — I'll leave the invitation open. We eat, you remember, about six-thirty."

"Thanks, Kev — I'll come if I feel up to it."

"Otherwise, you're alright?"

"Yes, I'm fine."

"*Now go away and leave me alone*," he thought silently.

"See you, then. Take it easy."

Andrew replaced the receiver without responding.

He did watch television that night — oddly, Kevin's phone call had made him determined to enjoy himself and choose what he wanted to watch, guilty feelings or not. He had a new kind of freedom and surely, the love of his life would want him to exercise it.

He did little over the Easter weekend — his parents had tentatively invited him back to East Anglia, but family and friends were not top of his agenda right then. He indulged himself in choosing and watching *his* favourite programmes on television, as well as the occasional trip to an out-of-town pub, though not again to the distant *Dog and Pheasant* — he doubted he could find it again anyway. In addition, embarrassment at seeing the landlord again was the main reason for the lack of a second visit. Trying to dismiss any guilty feelings that he was enjoying himself, he was beginning to realise that he had a new found freedom — freedom to do exactly what he wanted, at any time to suit him.

This self-indulgence was to be extended to an afternoon in a local bookies on Easter Monday afternoon. Arthur Bateman had first introduced him to betting on the horses and his mathematical skills had been of enormous benefit in calculating odds and winnings, if any. A couple of visits to Fakenham racecourse while courting Rachel had embedded the bug in his soul and also taught him much about his future father-in-law — he clearly gambled heavily and with some abandon at times. Little wonder that his supposedly thriving business seemed to struggle occasionally — at least according to Andrew's fiancé. Of all people, she knew how much went through the tills and what had to go out, but her father often insisted they were short of money. Rachel would question Andrew after each visit to Fakenham soon after the two men returned from their afternoon out together, which was always encouraged by her mother as a way of creating a bond between them. By the time they were due to be married, Rachel suspected that her father gambled heavily but she didn't have the heart to confront him, or tell her mother about it — it would have broken her heart to think that her husband had kept his 'secret' from her for so many years. In the end, with her and Andrew moving away from the family nest, Rachel tried to forget about it, praying that her dad would see the error of his ways before it was too late.

Andrew was well aware of his wife's opinion on gambling and having moved to Shropshire, he never again was to visit a racecourse while she was alive. However, latterly, particularly after Rachel's diagnosis, he had made one or two secret visits to the bookies, though always during the lunch hour while at school in Camton Magna. The gambling had never been too heavy, just enough to be hidden in other spending from their joint bank account. It was a secret he was not really proud of, given how much he and Rachel adored each other.

That Easter Monday gave him the opportunity to exercise his freedom still further without the secrecy that had encompassed his previous visits to *Bob Devlin's Racing* in Camton Magna's High Street. He put any feelings of guilt well to the back of his mind — he had become strangely relaxed about his vice. Why shouldn't he indulge? He could afford it, after all — his Head of Faculty's salary was almost too much for his needs, now that he was single again. Rachel had worked part-time in Market Camton's Post Office and most, if not all, her wages had been for her own disposal. He had always paid the mortgage and bills out of his salary and, now there was no mortgage, he had money to burn to satisfy a passion that his father-in-law had fuelled all those years previously. He had just sent off the relevant forms to cash in the life policy that would settle the outstanding mortgage on *Rose Cottage* and he had realised, perhaps for the first time that very morning that he would have at least £600 spare each month — to do with as he wished. As he drove to Camton Magna just after one that afternoon, he felt like a little boy again heading for Woolworth's in Hamsden or the sweet shop at the corner of Ferry Lane in Canford. He had drawn the maximum £500 from the Western Shires' ATM in Pig Lane earlier that day.

The bookies was crowded and uncomfortably warm — the weather had improved for the Easter Weekend, the last one in March and temperatures were well into the sixties. Bob Devlin had not, unfortunately, turned off the heating in his compact premises.

'*If you're not sure, or if you're late to the races, always back number one in the first race, Andrew, lad.*'

Arthur Bateman's words came back to him as he entered the den of iniquity. Glancing at the screens, he could see that the 1.50 race at, of all places, Fakenham was seconds from the off. He noted the name of the top horse. Grabbing a pen and slip, he scribbled his bet:

£50 win

Carsley's Surprise *1.50 Fak.*

Turning back to the screens, with the tapes about to be broken, he took in the price of his selection — 5/2 favourite. He recalled further words from his father-in-law:

'*Not top weight for nothing, not top weight for nothing, son.*'

He smiled — the memories of a Norfolk bonding came back to him and he felt warm inside. This had to be right. The venue for the race had to be an omen; he clutched his slip excitedly. The two-mile maiden hurdle was over in about four minutes and the favourite romped to victory, going clear before the last. Andrew had won £175, including his stake — £125 clear profit. Collecting his money from a rather attractive female assistant, he walked over to the details of the next races pasted on the walls of the shop. Towcester at 2.05 was another two-mile hurdle — but this time a handicap with eleven runners. His mathematical brain sprung into action and further advice came back to him:

'*Always choose a horse that is half-way down the betting in a handicap of eight or more runners, and back it each-way.*'

Andrew looked up at the screens and counted down to the fifth horse in the betting. His heart raced a little faster when he saw the name: *Dreaming of Marie*, priced at 8/1. Rachel's middle name was Mary and he really had been dreaming of her in the last few days. He wrote his bet out more carefully this time:

£50 E/W

Dreaming of Marie *2.05 Towcester*

There were two windows to place a bet at and he made for the one with the good-looking blond. Andrew slid his slip and five twenties through the hatch. The girl seemed to stare at him for longer than was appropriate.

"Thanks, Mr Grey — hope it wins for you, sir."

"What? Oh, yes, thanks."

He grabbed his slip and retreated to a far corner of the shop, almost out of the girl's eye line. He was sweating and his face felt hot. He hadn't recognised the girl but he guessed she had to be a former student from Castlemount Grammar. He made up his mind — he would leave after the present race. He didn't want any embarrassing questions. Maybe she knew his wife had just died. What would she think of him indulging in such a habit, especially so soon after his loss? Would she tell anyone at the school — other current pupils, or worse, a member of staff? That might not go down too well, given his leave of absence. So what, he suddenly thought — he was on a genuine holiday now, like every other member of staff.

Fortunately, *Dreaming of Marie* came in fourth and though he had lost £100 of his profit, he was saved the possible embarrassment of going to collect any winnings. He actually was out of the bookies before his horse had jumped the second last hurdle — it was trailing the third placed horse by more than twenty lengths.

As he strode quickly to his car, the feelings of guilt returned. What on earth was he doing? He was supposed to be a respected and respectable senior teacher. He had to get out of Camton Magna to think — the day was pleasant enough for a long walk. He had to clear his head and take control of his life which was rapidly being controlled by grief and the need to find a structure he could cope with. At the moment, he was alternating between a rebellion against his guilt of being alive and the self-indulgence to enjoy himself after nearly two years of darkness. He was living a life of extremes. There had to be a middle way, structured around the routine of school, perhaps. That was what he needed. He would be alright when he returned for the summer term, he assured himself. Right now, however, he felt lost, unable to enjoy anything without feeling guilty. Of course, if he could just go and talk to friends, like Kevin and Sally, he might feel better, but even that seemed futile when they had no idea what he was going through. Though it had only been just over two weeks, he'd already had his belly full of their platitudes. They meant well, but the problem was that Kevin and Sally had been too close to him and Rachel. They knew him too well — or, at least, they thought they knew him. No one knew or understood him at the moment — what he wanted or what he was capable of. Only one person really understood, and she was gone.

"Oh, please come back, Rachel!"

He had just got into his car and he had shouted the words as loudly as he could. No doubt, if someone had been passing, they could not have failed but hear them. He buried his head in his hands and cried uncontrollably. He sat back and tried to focus his streaming eyes. He had to clean his slate and rid himself of his guilt at being alive. For reasons he could not explain, he was overcome with the need to do penance, almost like the monks of old. He needed to cleanse his soul — to purify himself and restart his life on an even keel. He started the car and headed away from the town in the opposite direction to Market Camton. A long walk in the country, long enough for it to hurt, was his intention.

Five miles out of Camton Magna, he found a lay-by with a footpath sign beside it. He parked the Focus, donned the walking boots he always kept in the boot, and set out. It was twenty to three. He would walk until four and then retrace his steps to the car. He knew he was so out of condition that even an hour's walking would be difficult, let alone the three he was intending. It should be nearly dark by the time he returned and, hopefully, the euphoria born out of hard physical exercise would carry home and provide him with a relaxing evening in front of the television.

At first, the going was relatively easy and the path well marked across a series of flat fields with stiles linking them. When the gradient started to rise, he began to breathe heavily and his pace slowed. The path became indistinct and, on more than one occasion, led into impenetrable thickets which he had to back out of. Four o'clock seemed to come quickly — he was frustrated with his inability to follow the correct path, if indeed there was one. From his vantage point half-way up a grassy knoll he could still see the road in the distance, marked by the occasional headlights of passing cars in the onset of the dim late afternoon light. At least he had some beacons to guide him back if it got really dark. However, it had hardly been the serious expedition he'd intended — he gauged he was no more than three miles from his starting point. He felt some what deflated and charged himself with returning as fast as his legs would carry him. Twisted ankles or grazed shins would be ignored as he sought to carry out his punishment. It needed to hurt. The he might feel better.

It took him exactly forty-five minutes and it *did* hurt. A sore knee from a fall; mud up above his ankles; numerous scratches and legs that felt like jelly contributed to the euphoric feeling he'd hoped for but had dared not assume. Despite his near exhaustion, he felt good — better than he'd done for many days. It was a real effort to change back into his shoes as every muscle in his body seemed to ache. As he sat in the car in the gathering twilight, he reflected on the new found freedom that he'd abused in recent days. What he had just done was infinitely more beneficial for his health and well-being. Indeed, he thought, he was free to pursue other kinds of physical activity — activities that he liked doing but had been unable to take part in while Rachel had been alive, either owing to his role in her caring or the time it took out of their lives when she had been well. He hadn't played cricket for some years, when his wife had helped with the teas for the Market Camton XI. However, she had not liked him going on the away games when often he was away from lunchtime on a Saturday — or Sunday — until late into the evening. The season was about to begin and he imagined that practice sessions would be starting in the next week or so. At least it would occupy his Wednesday evenings during the summer and he might get his position back as Market Camton's wily swing bowler. Surely Rachel could not object to this use of his new freedom?

4

A Second Honeymoon

In preparation for returning to school and the hustle and bustle of human contact, Andrew decided to take up his friends Kevin and Sally's open invitation for dinner on the last Thursday before he was due back on the following Monday. He hadn't so far felt able to cope with the direct closeness of familiar faces but knew that without such a preliminary exercise he would find the following week difficult. Other than the necessary visits to local shops and a couple of excursions out of the village to anonymous pubs, he had said little to anyone — even the inevitable phone calls from Kevin and his mother had been brief and somewhat tortured. He just knew he had to get out that Thursday evening and try to emerge back into society. He was as nervous about returning to Castlemount Grammar as he had been all those years previously when he'd first set foot in Middleton High. He felt like a probationary teacher all over again — all confidence gone with only his academic knowledge for support. At least Castlemount's Head teacher, Mr John Dexter, was a wise man and had taken Andrew aside at Rachel's funeral to tell him that he was only going to be teaching his sixth form groups for the summer term. With only six weeks before all his groups were due to go on study leave for AS and A-levels, Andrew realised that he would have little to do — and that would be mainly revision classes. However, he wasn't altogether sure that he could even cope with those. His confidence was all but shattered beyond repair. He hadn't even tried to make contact with the local cricket club — something that he had promised himself he would do as a matter of urgency after his long walk.

At precisely six-thirty, Andrew rang the bell of number 17 Church Lane. Kevin Simpson opened the door immediately — it was clear he had been standing behind it, waiting expectantly and anxiously for his friend.

"Andy — good to see you, mate."

He shook Andrew's hand vigorously. Sally was in the kitchen putting the final touches to what looked like a sausage casserole. She wiped her hands on her apron and rushed to hug her husband's friend.

"Oh, Andy, I'm so glad you've come. We've been so worried about you."

She kissed his cheek and said,

"You two go into the lounge — dinner will just be twenty minutes."

Like Rachel and Andrew, the Simpsons were childless — a fact that had drawn Rachel to Sally in the first place about eight years previously. The difference, however, was that Sally was only thirty-three to her husband's thirty-eight and they had time on their side. With Kevin being a main scale History teacher and Sally a part-time cook in the school kitchens, they also had not yet reached the financial stability to embark on raising a family, much as they both wanted children.

Kevin led his friend into the small and cluttered lounge — he seemed as nervous as Andrew who took the initiative in opening the conversation.

"So, did you have a good Easter, Kev?"

"Yeah, not bad — we had Sally's parents over from Camton Magna on the Sunday. Spent most of the rest of the time working on the jungle that we call a garden."

"I've not touched mine yet. Apart from the lawns, Rachel looked after the rest. *She* was the gardener; I just obeyed her instructions."

'*And now I don't have to*,' he mused silently.

Kevin looked away at the first mention of his friend's late wife. It suddenly struck Andrew that perhaps other people were experiencing grief, too. He had been too self-indulgent and full of self pity to see how Rachel's death might have affected friends like Sally and Kevin. He reached across and placed a hand on Kevin's knee. He felt in control of a situation he thought he'd never be able to deal with.

"It's O.K., mate, I am able to talk about her, you know."

"Yeah, I'm, I mean, we're glad. Sal's been really worried about you. Says she often doesn't see your car on the track next to the cottage of an evening. I told her that you had every right to go for a drive, now that it's light until nearly eight."

So Sally had been checking up on him. How much further had she taken her investigations? He felt a little guilty, but also quite angry that a so-called friend should take it on herself to try and discover what he had been doing. It was his private life, after all. On the other hand, perhaps her concern was only natural — Sally and Kevin would pass *Rose Cottage* two or three times a day and would find it difficult not to glance his way. What really bothered Andrew at that moment, however, was the fact that she had felt the need to tell her husband and, indeed, the fact that Kevin had mentioned it to him. He tried to change the conversation, remembering how Rachel used to comment on Sally's 'big nose' as she would put it. Indeed, now he recalled it, she and Sally hadn't really been that close as friends. It had been he and Kevin, who saw each other every day, who had been good mates.

"So, is there anything I need to know before Monday, Kevin?"

"No, not really — briefing at 8.30 as usual. I think there's a Head of Faculty meeting on Tuesday after school, while we foot soldiers have year team meetings."

"I wish I was a foot soldier again," said Andrew quietly.

"Really?"

"Yeah, suddenly school seems so unimportant to me, Kev."

"That's understandable, Andy, for heaven's sake."

"Is it?"

"Of course — I think a lot of people thought you'd never come back, mate. You and Rachel were …."

"Were?"

"So close, so much in love, Andy."

"Yeah, too much in love. I loved her too much, Kev."

"You can't love someone too much."

"Can't you?"

"It's natural you should feel that way. God it's been less than a month."

"I know, and maybe I'm expecting too much of myself, but …."

"But what?"

Andrew paused and looked at his friend.

"I'm dreading going back on Monday. I'm not sure I'll be able to cope."

"You'll be alright, chief. The kids will good for you and the staff will support you. Dexter held an assembly after Rachel died to let all the school know of your loss and to tell them how committed you were and how much courage you had shown over the last eighteen months. Hardly any of the pupils knew of Rachel's illness and I think it came as a shock when he told them she'd passed away. There was an audible gasp in the hall when he announced it. A couple of the sixth form girls shed some tears. You seem to have forgotten how well liked you are at Castlemount."

"Oh, I didn't know JD was going to make it public. I'm not sure that was such a good idea."

"He had to, mate. Just think how awkward it could have been for you if say a pupil of yours started questioning you as to why you'd had time off. Better that the whole school has the same information and is prepared for your return. It'll help you in the long run. In fact, knowing most of our kids, they'll treat you with kid gloves — you'll have no discipline problems. You'll be fine, mate."

"I suppose so, but I don't want any favours. I just want to return to how it was."

"And you will — in time."

Andrew looked away from his friend. And that was the problem, wasn't it, he told himself. It was going to take time, a lot of time, and did he really want to go through that process, just as he had done eighteen years before when he'd first started out on his career?

"Dinner's ready!"

Sally's interruption broke his thoughts as he followed Kevin back into the kitchen that doubled as a dining room.

Andrew and Kevin spent a couple of hours in *The Royal Oak* that evening — neither was able to down more than two pints after Sally's filling meal. The conversation was bland, centred mainly on the coming cricket season and news that Sally's mother and father were thinking of moving to Scotland to be near some old friends who ran a guest house north of Inverness. Kevin spent quite a time relating his wife's feelings of abandonment, even though her parents currently lived the other side of Birmingham, on the outskirts of Rugby. Like she kept telling him, Kevin said, Rugby was more than eighty miles away, but at least you could be there in less than two hours. As for the north of Scotland, well that was a day, or more — and it was a different culture. For his part, Andrew did a lot of listening, while his friend unburdened himself of that and other of

Sally's worries, including her nagging him about having a baby. At the end of the evening, as Kevin left him at his front gate, Andrew pondered that it had always been that way — Kevin talking, and him listening. That particular evening he'd actually wanted to talk to Kevin but couldn't seem to find the right words to express his current feelings of apprehension about the coming term. Despite Kevin's earlier assurance that he would be fine, his nervousness was part of a general lack of confidence and included worries about where his life was going to go next. He knew that Sally would have wanted him to carry on as normal and enjoy himself, but every time he had tried, the burden of guilt returned. At that moment in time, he just couldn't see a way forward. He felt trapped and overwhelmed by the need to run away to another place where nobody knew him and where he could be himself, whatever that meant. He just didn't know who he was or who he was supposed to be. Half his life had been wiped away and what was left didn't seem to have any structure or motivation. He knew, when he sat down in the empty lounge that night, he would drink himself to sleep and half a bottle of his favourite whisky did the trick, blotting out the feelings of utter hopelessness that were filling his waking moments.

By the time Monday morning arrived, he had put those feelings to the back of his mind. He had a job to return to — he had to earn money to live and this pragmatic view of his future got him through the first day. He only had one group, the top set in Year 13 and they were still working through past papers that had been set by his number two, Joan Hanson, a divorced thirty something mother of two. He hardly had to answer a question from the six boys and three girls — all seemed reluctant to trouble him and he was continually conscious of the sad smiles that seemed to fill their faces whenever he occasionally addressed one of them.

Only Gary Thompson came up to him at the end of the lesson and said quietly,

"It is nice to have you back, Sir; we felt lost without you. Mrs Hanson is alright, but she …."

Andrew had put a finger to his lips to stop his best student saying something unprofessional about one of his colleagues and Gary merely nodded and left.

By the end of the week, and despite his light timetable, Andrew found himself driving back to Market Camton totally exhausted, both mentally and emotionally. Nevertheless, he was in quite a euphoric mood — if he could get through one week, he could get through another and there were only another five up to half-term. Then there would be no teaching for several weeks. It was a beautiful April evening and the thought of a weekend in which he was free to do exactly what he wanted cheered him enormously. Something to eat, followed by a drive in the country and finishing with just a couple of pints in a country pub was how he would spend the first evening of that free weekend. There hadn't been many occasions since Rachel's death when he had felt like this and he was going to make the most of it. He remembered what Rachel's GP had said about the highs and lows associated with grief. The lows would take you as low as any person could be taken but the highs often gave you pleasure greater than that ever experienced by normal grief-free people. The evening felt like it was going to be one of those heightened pleasurable events.

Over the next five weeks, the Friday evening drive was to become a regular occurrence for Andrew. He would deliberately choose a different pub each time, well away from Market Camton or Camton Magna. He whiled his time away playing the fruit machines, steering clear of being drawn into any conversations with the locals. No one knew him and he didn't have to act the part of a senior and highly respected member of the educational community. He was just and ordinary working man, like all the other regulars in the pubs he visited. Though he was still on his honeymoon period, as JD put it, school went well and he threw himself into helping his sixth form students with extra revision classes. It felt good to be back in the classroom where he'd always been respected as a caring teacher. Stocktaking and the following year's staffing gave him the chance to ease himself back into his administrative duties, even helping Deputy Head, Colin Davison, with some general timetabling duties as well. Thoughts of any serious physical exercise were put on the back burner until the May half-term where, on a sudden impulse, he decided to attend the practice nets at the village cricket field at the very end of Church Lane. It had been nearly seven years since he had played regularly but he still recognised some of the old familiar faces, though a good half of the players appeared to be of secondary school age. Fortunately, there was none from Castlemount in attendance that evening. Club Captain, Maurice Arnold spotted him immediately and 'Big Mo' ambled over to him as soon as he arrived.

"Andy, boy, it's good to see you. Come to turn your arm over again?"

"Thought I'd give it a try, Mo."

"Well you're more than welcome. We're short of a good bowler or two. Sorry to hear about your wife. I hope we can help you enjoy your cricket again."

"Me too, Mo."

But Andy didn't enjoy his cricket that evening. He just couldn't put a ball on a length and he had lost much of his speed and the ability to move it off the seam. After less than an hour, his shoulders and back ached beyond what he could bear. He fared no better when Mo invited him to have a bat. He'd never been a batsman and after another ten minutes of embarrassment where he managed to lay his bat on about one ball in three, he took off his pads and walked quietly off the field. Big Mo followed him back to the exit to Church Lane and, putting a burly arm round his tired shoulders, said,

"It'll take time, Andy, but it'll come back to you."

Andy said nothing and continued his embarrassed walk back home. It had been a bad idea — he was getting too old to bowl and he wasn't fit. God knows what he would be like in the field with so many players less than half his age seemingly available for the club. His ignominy was complete when, on Friday evening, Big Mo phoned to ask him if he would like to score for the village team — they could use his mathematical brain over the next few weeks, he said. Andrew declined gracefully. He wasn't yet quite ready for such a sedentary occupation that was normally associated with schoolboys or gentlemen of advancing years. He would have to find another pursuit to spend his free time on.

5
Solitary Pleasure

June moved slowly into July with Andrew only having two Year 12 groups to teach after their return from their AS exams. As was to be expected at that time of the year, neither group was particularly motivated to extend their learning, despite Andrew's encouragement that they needed to get a sizeable chunk of the A-level syllabus covered. With their more relaxed attitude, Andrew found himself returning to his less formal self — the teaching style that had made him such a popular teacher at Castlemount. Rachel's death had made him unable to engage with his students as freely as he had done before and he had adopted the role of lecturer rather than teacher prior to half-term. With his students' relaxation he felt more able to laugh and joke with them as he had always done in his career. However, one Monday morning at the beginning of July brought a jolt to his recovery. It was about ten minutes before the end of his class with the top set and he had just made a ghastly mistake in demonstrating the solution to an A-level problem. Steven Burley was quick to comment on his teacher's faux pas.

"Whoops, Sir! That's most unlike you. Been to the pub again, eh?"

Andrew's cheeks blushed as it suddenly hit him that his joking attitude could rebound on him. Normally he would have dismissed the comment with some sarcastic rebuff that was nevertheless sternly delivered. It would have said: '*You don't ask questions like that*,' and Steven Burley would have retreated back into his shell with his teacher having redrawn the line in the sand which the students knew they must not cross. But Andrew didn't, as he moved towards the edge of the hole that had been dug for him.

"I don't have time to go drinking, Steven, and I trust you know that you're too young to go to pubs, young man."

"*I* am," replied Burley with a smile. "But my dad isn't and he says he saw you in one last Friday evening."

He paused.

"And he says he tried speaking to you but you seemed a bit worse for wear."

Andrew was angry now — as angry with himself for letting the interrogation continue as he was with his student for being so impertinent. He was almost in the hole — but not quite, he thought. There was just a chance he could save face before he fell head first to the bottom. He suddenly was able to recall a couple of conversations he'd had with Mr and Mrs Burley at previous parents' evenings. His grim face broke into his '*I was only teasing*' grin.

"Now tell me, Mr Burley, what does you father do for a living?"

It was Steven's turn to look embarrassed.

"He's a clergyman, Sir," interjected Aaron Madison. "He's the vicar at St Jude's in town."

The rest of the twelve-strong class giggled. Andrew had pulled himself back from the gaping jaws of total humiliation. Steven Burley tried to mutter something about his father's flock being everywhere but his moment of superiority had gone. Andrew had re-established the teacher-student boundaries. He walked over to Steven and said quietly,

"And, yes, I did have a few relaxing pints last Friday evening but there are certain things that are off limits at school as far as you are concerned, and a teacher's private life is one of them, O.K? Sometimes it is better not to say anything especially if your only intention is to cause embarrassment. Was that your intention, Steven?"

"No, Sir — sorry, Sir. I was out of order."

“Apology accepted — we’d better leave it there today. I’ll see you all on Wednesday afternoon.”

Andrew flopped into his chair — it had been an ordeal he could have done without, even though it had been largely his own fault. He had responded initially like a probationary teacher. What was going on? Was he losing it? He sighed and looked up from his desk — he’d assumed all the class had gone, but two students stood nervously in front of him. Steven Burley and Joanne Cashman had something to say.

“Yes, guys?”

“Sir?” Joanne began.

“Yes, Jo,” replied Andrew sympathetically. Were his two weakest students going to ask if they could give up A-level?”

“Sir, we just wanted to say how really privileged we are to have you as our teacher after what you’ve been through. Most of us honestly thought you wouldn’t come back this term.”

Joanne Cashman paused and the deflated Steven Burley took over.

“And we’re truly pleased you did, Sir, and ….”

“And, Steven?”

“And I think you’ve every right to get drunk every night if you want to, Sir. My dad’s was concerned about you, Sir, that’s all and I shouldn’t have taken his comments out of context.”

Andrew could feel the tears welling up inside him. He needed to get some fresh air, and quickly. His students seemed to understand and were almost out of the room before he had a chance to say,

“Thanks for your understanding, Joanne and Steve.”

After they had gone, Andrew took his room key and locked the classroom door. He returned to his seat and spent the next five minutes weeping uncontrollably — it had taken two of his weakest students to give him a bigger lift than any of his friends and family had been able to manage over the past three or four months. '*Out of the mouths of babes and ….*'

It had been one of the 'highs' — in fact, when he got home that Monday night he felt invigorated and at one with himself for the first time since his loss. Life felt good; he was still a respected and much loved teacher and a celebration felt in order. He turned on his television and checked the racing teletext and his luck was in — there was an evening flat meeting at Wolverhampton, a track he'd never been to, even though it was only about forty-five miles from Market Camton and, along with Ludlow, was his nearest. The evening was warm and fine, with hardly a breath of wind, and though the racing would be fairly poor in class, his bank account was healthy and it would certainly avoid any further unfortunate meetings with parents if he had decided to celebrate in a liquid way instead. For no apparent reason, other than he was now in a position to do it, he had over a thousand pounds in cash in the cottage.

After a quick shower and change of clothes, Andrew was soon heading up the A5 to join the M54 for the run down to Wolverhampton. With any luck, he should be there by about 5.45, given that most of the rush hour traffic would be heading in the opposite direction away from the Birmingham conurbation. The first race of the seven-race card was scheduled for 6.05. He would grab some fish and chips when he got there — he was ravenous, having hardly eaten a bite at lunchtime after his 'chat' with Steven Burley.

On arrival at the compact all-weather track, he had no time to get any food as the first race was only five minutes from the start and the nine horses were already down at the start. According to his hastily purchased race card, it was Division 1 of a six furlong sprint for maiden fillies — the kind of race to be avoided, according to many of the media experts. But he was there to enjoy himself, and remembering Arthur Bateman's old adage, he rushed to the closest bookie and called out casually,

"A hundred on number one, please."

"Yes, sir, that's a ton on one."

Andrew took the computerised receipt — he hadn't even glanced at the board to check the horse's price. Now he looked down at his betting slip. If *Celtic Flyer* won he would be returned £350 at odds of 5/2 — it was second favourite to a John Gosden trained and Johnny Evans ridden filly called *Run With The Wind*. He held out little hope for his nag as the favourite was priced at 1/2 and shortening all the time. Even placing another £100 on it would not therefore recoup his stakes. He sighed and headed for the nearest food outlet. With punters already in their positions for the race, he was the only one waiting to be served. He managed to purchase his cod and chips quickly enough for him to be back on the tarmac apron in front of the Grandstand just in time to hear the racecourse commentator say,

"*All in; orders and off*!"

About forty-five seconds later, the writing was on the wall for *Celtic Flyer* as the favourite swept past imperiously at the two furlong marker. A little over twenty seconds and John Gosden's horse had won by six lengths with Andrew's selection fading badly in the last furlong to finish a disappointing seventh. '*Oh well*,' he thought, '*you can't win them all.*' Unfortunately, he didn't have a winner in any of the next three races, — not even a placed horse, and he was over £400 down. He decided that it was time for a side bet at one of the other evening meetings. He headed for the on-course betting hall where the 7.50 at Sandown was just minutes away. This time, he studied the form carefully — it was an eight-runner handicap over one mile and four furlongs. The favourite was an attractive

4/1 and the fourth horse in the betting was 17/2. The decision was easy for him — £50 each way at odds of more than 8 to 1. It only had to finish third to show a good profit of over £50. Of course, if it won, there would be over £600 to come back, and he would be up on the evening overall. Even the name of his selection seemed to be an omen — *On The Up* seemed more than appropriate given how he felt.

It was warm and sticky in the betting hall and finding a position where he could watch the race on the SIS monitors was no easy matter, as he was jostled left and right by anxious punters pushing past to get their last minutes bets on.

"Where's yow money, mate?"

The accent was pure Black Country. Castlemount had one or two ancillary staff that spoke like it, especially when they got excited or angry with the pupils — or teachers.

"*On The Up* — Eddie Ahern's mount," replied Andrew, comfortably. How easy it was to strike up conversations with total strangers at race meetings. The 'Sport of Kings' was a great leveller for rich and poor alike.

"It's got a chance, if 'e holds it up at the back."

"And you — what are you on?"

"Not had a bet in this one. I'm waiting for the next race here at Dunstall Park — had a tip from someone at the stables."

The last couple were entering the stalls.

"Yeah?" asked Andrew, trying to disguise his interest.

"The bottom weight is reckoned to be a good thing and it's well out of the handicap. Oi'm gonna' to lump on."

The man seemed to have got the information off his chest, as if being 'in the know' had given him some kind of superiority over the ordinary punters. He winked at Andrew and sidled away with an air of '*I know something that you don't know.*' Andrew opened his programme and made a mental note of the name of the bottom horse in the race — *Coppertop*. No omen in there, then. He didn't know anyone with ginger hair. The suggested odds were 16/1 and it was the horse's first time out. With an apprentice on board, and being out of an unfamiliar local yard, didn't bode well, but with '*horses for courses*' echoing in his head, he stuffed the race card in his back pocket and moved closer to the screens.

"*Last one going forward. Stand by.*"

On The Up was slow away, either by accident or design, and Ahern moved him quickly to the inside at the rear of the field as they climbed the notorious Sandown hill for the first time. The pace was a strong one, and by the time the horses had reached the back straight, there were a good twelve lengths from first to last. Andrew's horse was still to the rear, being waited with as the friendly tipster had suggested. With three furlongs to go, and just the straight and the hill to negotiate, Eddie Ahern 'pressed the button' and *On The Up* surged forward on the outside. Unfortunately, by then, two horses had opened up a lead of a good six lengths, and though Andrew's horse closed to within a length at the line, it finished only third. At least he had something to collect — £156.25 by his calculation. It was a start at getting some of his money back.

He only just about made it back outside in time to place a bet on the tip he'd been given by the Black Country stranger. The 8.05 race was due off in less than two minutes when he approached the line of bookies' stands in front of the Grandstand. He'd already made his mind up as to his bet — and though he exercised a little caution in the type of bet, he did not with the stake.

"£250 each way on number eleven, please."

Reg Martin looked down from his position on his box and said,

"*How* much, sir?"

Andrew repeated his bet.

"Well alright, sir, but on your head be it. She's no chance."

"We'll see, mate," replied Andrew.

"Ah, got a tip, eh?"

Andrew said nothing and handed over the wad of notes. The bookie handed them to his assistant to count — the operation seemed to be accomplished in impossibly quick time.

"All correct," came the response.

"Good luck, sir," said the bookie.

Andrew walked away and looked excitedly down at his betting slip. He had just wagered the largest amount ever, but the potential returns were staggering. The price was better than expected — 20/1, and his winnings, if *Coppertop* was to come home first, would be £6500; £5250 for the win and £1250 for the place. A new car beckoned, he thought.

The engine of his Nissan 350Z alternated between its cruising purr to a deep throaty roar as he pressed down on the accelerator to overtake slower moving traffic on the M6. It was mid-August and he was heading north for a weekend in the Lake District, ostensibly to do some walking but also to visit Carlisle and its small racetrack for a summer flat meting. He had attended several more race meetings since that first triumph at Wolverhampton: Ludlow, Warwick (twice) and Wolverhampton (three times) where he now felt he was a regular. The Nissan, though not brand new, had still set him back nearly £20000, and even part-exchanging the Focus it had left him £7500 short. The loan had been easy to obtain — he had no mortgage on the cottage. He'd taken out more than he actually needed for the car owing to some big losing bets he'd had in the first couple of weeks of August. He didn't care; he was enjoying himself — solitary pleasure, yes, but right then it was what he needed. Towards the end of term, he had got tired of the feelings of guilt. He only had one life, after all, and he was going to make the most of it. If he'd learnt one thing from Rachel's death at such a young age, it was that you had to live for the day.

He didn't do much walking that weekend — the pull of a Saturday afternoon at the races had been too strong. By the time he arrived back in Market Camton late Monday evening, he'd climbed just one minor 1500 foot high fell but lost another couple of grand as well. Depression set in again that week — it should have been a lesson well learnt but he was hooked on the vice that destroyed so many lives. The trouble was, his 'devil may care' attitude was beginning to rule his life, and the only way he could seem to relieve the guilt, boredom and 'lows' that continually overwhelmed him, was to gamble more. The excitement of a possible win was like a drug that deadened the 'bad' feelings, as he called them. He often asked himself what the alternative was. In his darkest moments, he'd considered that alternative, for sure, but the 'how' had scared him — he couldn't stand pain, even for the shortest of times. Thus it was that Andrew Grey was caught between extremes of solitary pleasure and bouts of depression. By the end of the month, he was desperately looking forward to getting back to work and the structure it had given his life the previous term, even though he would be facing a full timetable with new classes to teach.

6
Difficult Lessons

Further trips out were put on hold for the last two weeks of August as examination results had to be analysed and the new Year 12 groups organised. Andrew spent most days in school, revelling in the best GCSE and A-level results for some years. However, Head teacher, Mr Dexter lavished praise on his Head of Maths at every available opportunity, causing him much embarrassment at times. Kevin Simpson immediately nicknamed his friend as 'the Head's blue-eyed boy'. After the last staff meeting before term began, Kevin went one further as they strolled back to Andrew's new sports car in which they had both travelled to Camton Magna earlier that day.

"He's got you lined up for Deputy Head, you know, when Colin Davison retires in a couple of years. You're much cleverer than him anyway and would make a better fist of the timetable. Mine is awful this year — I mean, double Year 9 History on a Friday afternoon.

"Someone's got to have the slot. Mine's not too good either — I've given myself bottom sets in both Years 10 and 11."

"Yeah, but not after a single period with the same group in the same morning — all their History on one day. It'll make marking so difficult and I bet the Year 10 GCSE numbers are down next year. Just wait and see. Also, have you heard about Year 8 PE for 8L?"

"No," replied Andrew.

"Well, good old CJD has put it before lunch on Wednesday."

"So, it has to go somewhere."

"Yeah, but he's also put Year 8 Games that afternoon too — two showers in one day?"

"Tricky, Kev."

"Stupid, if you ask me — the poor little dears will be knackered by the time they go home. We had a much better timetable that year when you helped out and did it because CJD had pneumonia. You've been on a course as well, haven't you?"

"Yep, University of Bimingham — I remember it well. Rachel thought it was just another jolly for teachers. She didn't realise it was twenty hours of concentrated simulation squeezed into three days. It was exhausting, mate."

They had reached Andrew's car and Kevin, with a sly grin, remarked,

"It doesn't look as if it's been vandalised, Andy?"

"There are no pupils in today — all potential sixth formers have been interviewed and there are no remedial classes."

Kevin sniggered.

"I didn't mean by our students, I meant by our staff. Several of them are very envious of you."

Andrew turned to stare at his friend. Kevin knew at once he had said the wrong thing.

"Ah sorry, mate, I didn't think. How could they be envious of you — nobody would?"

"It's O.K., Kev, don't dig a bigger hole for yourself. I'm not the only bloke ever that has lost his wife."

"Yeah, but …."

"Leave it, Kevin. Let's get back to Market Camton."

"Yeah, and in one piece Jenson, if you please."

Andrew smiled as he gunned the accelerator and the 350Z sped out of the car park.

Though he had had lower sets before, it had been quite a time back in the early years of his appointment as Head of Department. Others had always seemed better suited to coping with them and he'd always used his subject prowess with the top sets — the sixth form in particular. But earlier that year, he thought he had sensed some unrest in the department about previous staffing arrangements. Consequently, he had decided to take two of the more challenging groups for the forthcoming year. He was always apprehensive during the last summer weekend before an autumn term started anyway, but this year he seemed even more so. Indeed, by Sunday night, he was getting really quite scared about taking the two groups, both of whom had created a reputation for themselves lower down the school. Why had he bowed to some vague murmurings? In addition, as the new term had approached, he had felt a waning in his confidence to teach, and memories of being a probationary teacher had flooded back. It felt like he was starting out again. He would drink more than a couple of whiskies that night as Monday loomed ever closer.

The second mini-honeymoon period lasted exactly two weeks. The first of several 'incidents' occurred on a Thursday morning with Andrew's Year 10 set 4. Though a smallish group, containing just 16 pupils, there was a couple that had had problems ever since they had started in Year 7. One, Marcus Bradbury, had been in foster care from the age of eight after his mother and father had been prosecuted and fined for neglect. The other, Matthew Johnson, was very small for his age, and his self-consciousness often revealed itself in anger and frustration at the other pupils' gibes and mickey-taking. Bradbury's question seemed innocent enough but it served its purpose in disturbing the other pupils' concentration.

"Nice car you've got, Sir."

“Yes, it is, Marcus, now please concentrate on what I’m doing. And put your hand up when you want to ask a question.”

Andrew paused while the rest of the class tried to control their sniggers.

“Now, the question was: what is the size of the angle inside a regular pentagon?”

Marcus Bradbury seized his chance. He dutifully put his hand up.

“Yes, Marcus?” said Andrew with a sigh. “Please enlighten us.”

“I don’t know, Sir, but I bet it’s bigger than Johnson.”

The group descended into fits of laughter and catcalling.

“Anything’s bigger than him!” shouted Amy Redfern.

Andrew stared at his class — the stare that always usually worked. He was not a shouter and he rarely lost his temper. The noise barely subsided.

“I’m waiting 10 set 4,” he said quietly.

Still they carried on. The majority of the class seemed to be ignoring him. It had been a long time since any group had done that. He was not going to be beaten. He walked down the centre of the room, neither looking left or right. At the back of the classroom, he turned and faced the front so that now he was behind every pupil. He said quietly,

“You have ten seconds in which to be silent.”

One or two of the girls turned round sheepishly, but the majority still ignored Andrew. He added in a voice that was struggling to control his anger,

“Or you’ll all serve a detention with me at lunchtime.”

One of the girls said,

“But that’s not fair, Sir — me and Cheryl haven’t said a word.”

By this time, Matthew Johnson had clearly had enough of the comments that were flowing freely. Brushing his books and pens to the floor, he stormed out of Room 52, banging the door loudly behind him.

"Ooh, Sir, Johnson's doing a runner!" shouted Amy Redfern.

Andrew was sweating. He looked at his watch — just five minutes left of the lesson. He would deal with Matthew Johnson later. He had to get his control back. He strolled to the front of the classroom and at last the class seemed to sense he meant business.

"Right that's it!" he shouted, completely deafening the nearest pupils. His face was red and contorted in anger. It was clearly apparent that they had never heard a teacher shout so loudly or so angrily, and they were caught totally by surprise — one or two even looked downright scared. Was this their highly respected, mild mannered and thoroughly nice teacher? There was almost immediate silence. Most pupils hung their heads and looked at their desks. A few, however, continued to stare at their teacher, their faces contained a mixture of pity and embarrassment for him. Andrew attempted to regain his composure, and in a more moderate tone, he continued,

"You have behaved abysmally this lesson and you will all report back here at one o'clock," and turning to the two 'innocent' girls, he added,

"And that includes all of you."

"But, Sir …."

"No buts — now, if you can, pack away silently and go to your next lesson."

To his relief, they more or less did as they were told, but Andrew noted the superior smirk that had appeared on Marcus Bradbury's face — and that on one or two of his 'cronies'. The sarcastic grin said, '*Now we know how to wind you up, this is only the beginning*'.

To his added relief, Matthew Johnson had not walked out of school but had reported himself to the main office, even though it was on the pretence of feeling sick. When Andrew got there after the end of the lesson with his abandoned books and equipment, his mother had already been notified and she was on her way to collect him. Questioning the senior secretary, it was clear that Matthew had not mentioned the name calling or his sudden desertion of the classroom. Fortunately, Susan Weeks assumed that Andrew had legitimately sent Matthew to the office. Andrew decided it was perhaps not the right time to correct that impression or to notify Mrs Johnson of the real reasons behind her son's 'sickness'. He would talk privately with Matthew on his return, including the possibility of a change of sets. Fortunately, he was about the brightest in the set and a good case could be made for promotion to set 3.

He was inevitably late for his next class — and luckily it was at the opposite end of the academic divide. His best group that year was his Year 13 Further Maths set, many of whom he'd taught from Year 7. He could always relax with them and share a mature joke or two, without being unprofessional — they knew the boundaries and worshipped him. This group contained his two favourite students — Steven Burley and Jo Cashman who between them had done so much the previous term to make him feel part of the school again. An hour with them lifted his spirits and it wasn't until he was sitting with 10 set 4 for their lunchtime detention, minus Marcus Bradley and two others, that he had a chance to reflect on his first difficult lesson in years. It had been a wake-up call. It felt like he needed to relearn all the standard techniques for dealing with unruly classes. Clearly the shouting and anger had worked that morning but he also knew the pitfalls it could lead to. The words of his PGCE tutor came back to him: '*Never lose your temper in class, Andrew. If you do, you've show them you've got a weakness and they'll exploit it*'.

He wouldn't have 10 set 4 again until the following Monday, but he was not looking forward to the experience. Something told him that he had much work to do if he and they were going to form a happy and stable relationship.

By the time half-term came at the end of October, Andrew had had two or three more 'incidents', as he was prone to call them amongst some of his colleagues. He was loath to discuss what he saw as he own deficiencies too openly, but along with Kevin there were one or two others he felt able to unburden his perceived problems at times. He was to be given some sound advice by one such colleague, his number two, Joan Hanson, albeit perhaps with one selfish eye on his job. They were alone together in the staff room at the end of school the second day back after the autumn break, generally relaxing and checking their mail. Andrew started to unburden himself a little after another earlier angry rant at 10 set 4, now minus Matthew Johnson, who had been moved up to set 3 to avoid any more problems with Marcus Bradbury.

"You know, Joan, I've been having some more problems with 10 set 4 and to a lesser degree 11 set 5."

"Two tough groups, Andrew," she replied.

"I know but I've had worse before."

"Yes, but not for a very long time, I suspect, and certainly not since I've been here and that's ten years next summer."

"Is it really?"

"Is there any thing I can do to help," she said sympathetically. "I could sit in on a lesson with you — my Year 10 top set can be left with one of the assistants for half an hour or so. Sometimes, they hardly know I'm there anyway they work so hard."

"You're lucky."

"Anyway," Joan continued, "it was never going to be that easy for you after …."

"I suppose not," replied Andrew — he could feel the tears welling up. It had been hard for him to broach the subject with another Maths teacher, especially one who had taught both groups before. Suddenly he felt inadequate.

"You know, I don't reckon I'm cut out for this game anymore."

"Nonsense, Andy, you're the best teacher at Castlemount — in any subject," she added.

"Well I don't feel like it and I certainly don't need the money now."

Joan Hanson leaned forward in her armchair. This sounded interesting.

"So what do you want to do?"

"I don't know yet, Joan, but only teaching sixth form somewhere appeals to me."

"What, you'd leave us for another school?"

"Maybe, or just teaching the sixth form here."

"Sounds like you need to go and talk to JD. It would mean going part-time — we wouldn't be able to staff the department at the moment given we're all fully loaded."

"I know, and I'm not sure that's what I want anyway. What would I do with all the extra free time?"

Joan leaned back and said,

"I still think you should go and see the Head, especially if you do decide on that path. He would need to know as early as possible in order to make plans for the future."

"Yeah, I suppose so. I was going to give it until Christmas anyway so I'll wait until then and then make a decision."

"I would still go and talk to him now. It can't do any harm."

Joan seemed strangely insistent as she repeated her advice.

"You're probably right, Joan. I'll go and see him soon."

But Andrew didn't go and discuss his problems with the Head and they got worse as the term approached Christmas. He was achieving little with 10 set 4; just keeping them quiet took all his time and effort. Marcus Bradbury seemed to spend more time in the corridor or outside the Deputy Head's office than in Room 52. Joan offered to take him and sit him at the back of her class but Andrew saw that solution as a further admission of failure. Given that there were two or three others, Amy Redfern included, who were becoming nearly as disruptive, he knew that removing individual pupils was not the answer. He had to conquer his shortcomings — or take drastic action. 11 set 5 were better but his perception was still that they were not progressing as they should — and he blamed himself almost entirely. The only thing that seemed to keep him from walking permanently out the school was the relaxation and safety he felt when with his sixth form groups. At the end of the first week in December, with just nine school days left until the end of term, Andrew decided that, if there was no improvement in that time, he would take Joan Hanson's advice and make an appointment to see the Head at the very start of the spring term.

7
Dark Thoughts

As ever, the last week of the autumn term was filled with carol rehearsals, services and house competitions, which meant that very little sensible teaching could be accomplished. Without much structure to his lessons, Andrew found his Year 10 and 11 classes even more difficult to handle. Try as he might to give them puzzles and other entertaining mathematical games, they ignored most of his invitations, preferring instead to chat to each other. In the end, he had to resort to basic 'crowd control', trying nothing more than to keep the noise at a reasonable level, so as not to disturb any neighbouring classes. Nevertheless, he received one or two polite enquiries from other staff concerning what had been going on in his lessons. As he drove back to Market Camton at the end of the penultimate day of term, he had a real sense that his problems were beginning to be discussed more openly by his colleagues — the odd sympathetic look across the staff room; conversations suddenly being curtailed when he got too close and a general perception that his honeymoon period was over.

He looked upward at the ceiling and between the sobs he cried,

"Oh God, help me! Show me what to do!"

He'd never been particularly religious and there had only ever been a handful of times in his life when he had uttered similar supplications. He was sitting in his lounge and he felt he was on the edge of a break down. It was dark now and he hadn't bothered to put any lights on. The blackness matched his mood and he felt helpless and afraid — afraid that his reputation was disappearing down the drain; afraid that he would never teach again and afraid that there was only one alternative to his desperation. He leant back in his armchair and tried to focus his mind. He had to do something about his situation and it had to be done quickly. Joan Hanson's advice floated in and out of his tortured mind.

'*I would still go and talk to him now. It can't do any harm.*'

And it couldn't he thought. So what if JD was unsympathetic? So what if he didn't listen? At least he would leave the Head in no doubt as to how he felt about his ability to cope with some classes. He rubbed his jacket sleeve across his eyes and reached over to turn a table lamp on. The sudden brightness stung his reddened eyes and he felt the stark reality of his position. He tried to reassure himself that all was not doom and gloom. His sixth form groups still respected him and worked hard for him. Maybe he could persuade JD to release him from his two GCSE bottom sets — there had to be a way, surely, hadn't there? He thumped the arms of his chair in anger and frustration.

"I will go and see him first thing tomorrow morning!" he shouted at the ceiling. "And hang the consequences — it's my life and I'm going to take control."

The outburst seemed to have a calming effect on him, but it was balanced by the need to blot out his dark thoughts. He just wanted it to be 8.30 the following morning. He wished he could turn the clock forward instantly and get what he had to say to the Head off his chest. He looked down at his watch, barely able to read the face in the dim light. It was 5.30 — he had fourteen and a half hours to wait; fourteen and half hours to kill; fourteen and a half hours in which to rescind his decision. He knew what he wanted to do — he had to drink himself to sleep. Sleep would shorten the time he had to wait. However, he didn't want to drink alone and he didn't want to do it anywhere near Market Camton or Camton Magna. Without a moment's thought for the consequences, he rushed upstairs to change into some casual, nondescript clothes. He knew exactly where he would go and he knew he could always get back by taxi, no matter how costly.

No Welshmen this time; in fact very few people were out and about on the roads that Thursday evening. It was cold, even for the week before Christmas, with the hedgerows already clothed in a white hoar frost. The drive had taken Andrew well over the hour, after he first missed the turning off the A458 and then drove right through the village of Ripley. After doubling back, he eventually found his preferred choice of pub in which to drown his sorrows. *The Dog and Pheasant* looked welcoming; with its festive lights adorning the outside and the real Christmas tree dominating the main bar. However, as soon as he stepped through the main door, he began to feel nervous and have some doubts as to whether he was doing the right thing. A moment's hesitation was quickly replaced by thoughts of the alternative — a drive back to Market Camton and the half bottle of whisky in his lonely cottage. He almost physically shuddered at the prospect and then, without another thought, strode into the brightly lit bar.

Though the roads had been largely free of traffic, the pub seemed to have drawn a goodly number to its welcoming log fire and seasonal atmosphere. As he strolled nonchalantly up to the bar, he observed that the clientele seemed to consist entirely of locals from the village, confirming what he had guessed from the virtually empty car park. He would hold onto his keys for as long as he could that night. His mood had lifted on the drive over and, as he sipped his first pint, he was hit with the realisation that it was human company he needed, more than drowning his sorrows and numbing his senses. He *would* drive home; he knew he could do it without drawing attention from the police. He would keep to *his* limit, even if it was way above what was generally considered to be safe. After all, he had that whisky to help him sleep. He was here to enjoy himself and to socialise as he wished.

Either the landlord didn't recognise him from nine months previously, or he did, but didn't want to embarrass his new customer.

"I bet it's cold out, isn't it?" he asked.

"Yes, there's a frost in the air," replied Andrew coolly.

"All ready for Christmas?"

"No, not yet. I expect you'll be busy."

"We're not opening Christmas Day but we've got a local band Christmas Eve; we'll be packed out then. We often have a sing-song with them, especially if any Welsh turn up."

The landlord winked at Andrew and turned to serve another customer. Andrew took a deep breath. So he had recognised him, he thought; time to move to a quiet corner, if he could find one. He did, but within a few minutes he found himself hemmed in by three other customers. At first, he didn't join in any of their conversation which seemed to centre on the arrangements for a golf foursome at the weekend. Golf had never been one of Andrew's favourite games. Other than some pitch and putt at the seaside when he had been a kid, he saw very little point in it and was very much of the opinion that it was '*a good walk spoiled*'. Eventually something one of them said sparked some interest in him.

"I wish we could get Henry out, you know."

"Yeah, he needs to take up with his friends again after his loss."

"Trouble is they were totally devoted to each other — went everywhere and did everything together. He's lost without her."

"Only fifty-one, you know."

"Was she? I thought she looked a lot older."

"That was the cancer and the chemotherapy."

“He’s aged too — looks over sixty now.”

Andrew’s heart was beating faster. He needed to find out more.

“What type of cancer did she have?” he asked of no one in particular, as he continued to gaze into his half empty glass.

“What, mate?” asked a rather fat bald man of about fifty.

Andrew looked up and held the man’s stare.

“What did she die of?”

“Lung cancer,” replied another thinner man whose name Andrew had gleaned was Tom. “Why do you ask, young fella’?”

Dare he? He hadn’t discussed Rachel’s death with anyone except his close friends or family. His answer came surprisingly naturally, almost as though he was in a discussion comparing what cars they drove.

“I’ve not long lost my wife to a brain tumour.”

All three men looked at him in silence. Andrew felt he needed to continue — the silence had become awkward.

“I’m O.K. now,” he lied. “It was back in March.”

Tom seemed interested in Andrew’s explanation.

“Really? Henry lost his Martha about then, didn’t he, Bill?”

“Yeah, it was about the 20th, I think.”

Only three days apart, thought Andrew. It had to be some kind of omen. However, the three men still seemed a little ill at ease. Andrew noticed that their glasses were all now empty

“Buy you a drink before we go?” said Tom.

“Oh, er, no I’m fine thanks,” replied Andrew.

“Right,” said Bill. “We’ll leave you in peace. Take care of yourself, young man.”

With that, and a few sympathetic looks, the three men moved quickly away to leave Andrew to think about his short conversation with them. His interruption had obviously been difficult for them to handle.

And think he did, but with very mixed feelings. It had cheered him to think that other people went through what he had been through, and that some one called Henry still felt totally lost without his soul mate. On the other hand, he felt a little guilty too that there were others who seemed to have fared worse than he had, even ageing by years in a few short months. He would have loved to have been able to talk to Henry — swap notes and exchange their tales of misery. It might have done them both good.

He'd had four pints of the local brew before he made his first excursion to relieve himself. He was surprised how quickly time had gone when he glanced at his watch as he stood in front of the urinal — it was already gone nine. As he turned to wash his hands, he couldn't avoid the large plate glass mirror above the wash basins. The thought of someone else ageing prematurely caused him to stare for longer than usual at his own face. His heart seemed to miss a beat as it occurred to him that *he* had aged too, especially around the eyes. They looked heavy and hollow and it wasn't just from the drink; he hadn't drunk that much yet anyway. The heaviness looked permanent. He was beginning to look old and somewhat haggard. Even a forced smile couldn't seem to hide the gauntness; the new lines and the vacant expression. He shuddered — it had only been nine months, and why hadn't he noticed the change in his appearance before? He stood facing his image, almost in disbelief that he could have missed the transformation. What was happening to him? Perhaps it was the fluorescent light above him. That had to be it — it was just too bright and artificial. He felt a little better — time for the whisky at home.

His depression returned as soon as he walked into the familiar surroundings of *Rose Cottage*. Even two quick large whiskies did little to raise his spirits. Dark thoughts shot like electricity through his head. He felt cold and very much alone, the shivering sensation fighting the alcohol in his bloodstream. As he sat in his chair long past midnight, the thoughts got darker and wilder. If he'd had a bottle of Paracetamol or other painkillers in the house, it would have been touch and go as to whether he could have resisted the 'temptation' to down them with the remaining whisky. In the end, he satisfied himself with the extra half bottle he'd purchased off the landlord as he'd left *The Dog and Pheasant*.

8
The Mission

They certainly looked high enough, though not as high as he remembered them as a child. He was sweating profusely, despite a coldness that seemed to envelop him. He peered over the edge — the sea was rough and the tide in. The water looked deep at the bottom of the cliffs. He was strangely calm; all fear of pain and failure gone from his mind. He just wanted to get it over with and there was a prize waiting for him at the other end. He would see his beloved Rachel again.

"No, Andy!"

Her voice seemed to echo in his head and it was insistent.

"No, Andy, it's not your time yet!"

"But I'm lost without you, love!" he cried out. "I don't want to go on."

"But you must; you're still young and you've so much to give as a teacher."

"I can't teach now; I'm no good!" he screamed this time.

The silence was broken only by the waves lapping at the foot of the cliffs. He covered his ears to shut out his wife's words. It would only take a few seconds, and if the fall didn't kill him, he would drown quickly beneath the waves. He took a pace forward, the tips of his feet hanging over the edge. He looked down — unseen hands seemed to be pushing him backwards. It made no difference as he hurled himself head first into oblivion. He could hear ringing in his ears. He screamed as he suddenly realised the irreversibility of what he had done.

"Oh, God, no!

The ringing got louder and had regularity to it. He was bathed in sweat — his head ached badly. He wasn't in real pain, though. Was this death? Had it been all that easy? Then he was awake and it suddenly dawned on him — it had all been a bad dream. He was still in bed at *Rose Cottage*, and not at Canford Cliffs near the village where he grew up. He felt awful — the worst hangover he could ever remember. The phone continued to ring. He pushed himself upright and reached for the receiver beside his bed. He dare not stand up. His heart was thumping. What on earth was the time? His bedroom was bathed in light. It had to be late.

"Ye-es?" he mumbled in a gruff voice.

"Mr Grey, it's Susan Weeks from school — Mr Dexter asked me to ring you as you're not in yet. Is everything alright?"

Andrew had to think quickly. There was no way on earth that he could go to school. His head was swimming and he was on the verge of being sick. He doubted he could even stand upright, let alone drive or walk. The room was still moving. He had to lie. He didn't need to put on a 'sick' voice as his hangover did it for him.

"Oh, I'm so sorry, Susan; I've had a bad night — a touch of flu, I think. I'll try to get in later. Wha-what's the time?"

"It's just gone ten. We suspected you had something — you didn't look well yesterday. No, Mr Grey, Mr Dexter has already arranged your classes so there's no need for you to come to school. We don't want you spreading any germs here before Christmas."

Andrew mumbled his thanks and he dropped the receiver before the school secretary had a chance to wish him a Merry Christmas. He collapsed backwards with the awful sensation that his bed was not going to prevent him from going right through it. He was torn between the need to visit the toilet to be sick and the realisation of the improbability that he could stand, let alone walk or even crawl there. In the end, he opted for lying as still as he could while he tried to gather his thoughts. Five minutes later and he had fallen back into a deep, dreamless sleep — it was definitely not going to be a Merry Christmas.

In the end, he wasn't sick that day — at least, not physically. Sleep preserved his numbness until well after lunch when he eventually managed to rise to empty his bladder. Of course, he felt dreadful, but his physical condition wasn't his main concern. Memories of the dream had come flooding back to him; something that rarely happened with him. He just couldn't shake off the thought that it had seemed so real — he *had* leapt from the cliffs at Canford, he was sure of it. It scared him to think that, even though it had been dream, he still had had the guts to end his life. He had *wanted* to do it.

As he sat in his favourite armchair, clutching a pint glass of water — his second one — designed to flush the alcohol from his system, he tried to clear his head of all bad thoughts. Rachel hadn't wanted him to join her. What had she said? Ah, yes, '*it's not your time yet*'. Had it been her time, then? Did everyone have a time? Did dying give you foresight? Did she know when he *would* join her? All these, and other questions, flew into and out of his brain without being answered. He had no answers to any of them, except for one, and that was what he was going to do there and then? He knew he had to get away, far away from *Rose Cottage*, Market Camton and the school. Fortunately he was free of the latter for over two weeks, but how did he get away from the other places. Where could he go? Should he ring JD and tell him about his problems? No, he would leave that till his mind was right, at the start of the spring term. Then, suddenly, he knew where he would go — indeed, where he needed to go.

At first, while he was motoring down the M54 and then the M6, he was fine. Then, when he reached the A14, with its early indications of towns towards and on the East Anglian coast, he became nervous about his intentions. He hadn't rung his parents to say he would be coming home for Christmas — he hadn't wanted to over excite them, just in case he got half-way and then decided to turn round and drive back to Market Camton. He'd used the rest of Thursday to recover, and to try to make himself presentable — two hot showers and a decent home-cooked meal of liver, bacon and onions had revived him considerably. Now it was the last Friday before Christmas, the 25th being the following Tuesday, and the option of turning round loomed large in his mind. Now that he had made his decision, he still wasn't really looking forward to spending Christmas with his parents, especially not his mother, who would fuss and flap over him. That wasn't the real reason he had to go back to Canford. He could have just booked into a hotel, but that would have provided the inevitability of spending long periods of time on his own, and he didn't want to get drunk again, just in case .... Being with his parents would be hard, but at least there would be people who could, and would, keep an eye on him. And it gave him the perfect opportunity to go to the place that he had made his sole and immediate mission.

By four, with the onset of twilight, he first noticed the signs to Cambridge — less than 60 miles to go, he thought. Having crossed one hurdle back at the start of the A14, another presented itself when he saw the first sign with his home village mentioned. Canford was small, but it still merited a place next to the bigger towns of Newmarket, Bury St Edmunds and Ipswich, put there, no doubt, because it was simply 'the end of the line'. The sight of the village of his birth and upbringing made him feel queasy again. Even stopping for a strong black coffee at a *Little Chef* just outside Bury could do little to rid him of his anxieties — only the thought of his 'mission' got him back into the 350Z to finish the last 30 miles or so.

It wasn't to be until after lunch on Christmas Day that he finally had the perfect excuse to set off for his target. The days leading up to the 25th had been filled with the preparations for the big day and several visits by and to old family friends and neighbours. He had felt warmed by their kind words, but also rather surprised to realise that so many people cared about him. Christmas lunch had been a quiet affair, with just the three of them sitting down to one of Gladys Grey's legendary meals. Andrew's dad, Percy, was soon asleep in his favourite chair, with little prospect of him stirring for at least a couple of hours. Andrew had joined him in the chair opposite when his mother came in from the kitchen to say,

"Andrew, why don't you get some fresh air and go for a walk. You look as though you need it and it's a sunny afternoon. Just be careful of the pavements — they are probably still quite icy."

A walk that afternoon hadn't been in his plans — he knew that he would be on his own the following afternoon as his parents had been invited to some friends in Ipswich, and he had deliberately excused himself from accompanying them on the pretext that he had never met them. Maybe he could go twice. He looked up at his mother and said,

"You know, Mum, I think I will. Walk off that lunch. Are you sure you don't want any help clearing up, though?"

"No, love, you get off — I can manage, and your dad won't be much company for you for ages. Where will you go?"

"I thought I'd head for Canford woods."

"Well, just be careful, you know those woods are haunted."

"Yeah, right, Mum. That's just an old wives' tale."

"Maybe, but it used to frighten you when you were a boy. They used to say that the ghosts of a couple of patients from the asylum still roamed free in the woods."

"Mum, for goodness sake, you'll believe anything you're told."

It took him less than ten minutes to find the path that led deep into the heart of the woods. At first, the going was easy, with the often muddy ground frozen quite hard and very little ground cover to slow his progress. After another half an hour, with his heart starting to pump faster, he began to hear the sound of the sea crashing against the cliffs — so the tide was in just like ….

"Just a coincidence," he muttered to himself.

He was sweating, even though he felt deathly cold. He shivered — he had to get it over with. Suddenly, a small clearing came into view — it was surrounded by trees, with just one small entrance in and out. Though he had been there many times as a boy, he couldn't ever recall seeing the slightly strange, almost fairy-like circular clearing, which appeared devoid of any grass or vegetation under foot. He squeezed himself through the narrow opening and slowly approached the far side which faced the cliff edge. It all looked and felt the same as in his dream. Was this his time? He called out over the raging sea beyond.

"Rachel, I'm here, love!"

The silence was deafening as he could hear his heart thumping in his chest. He waited and then shouted,

"Shall I come, Rachel?"

Still there was no response; just the moaning of the wind in the trees. Suddenly, he thought he could hear other voices which seemed to come from directly in front of him.

'*Come and join us! Come and join us*!'

‘*Us*’, he thought. What did that mean? Was there more than one person calling to him? Then his mother’s words came back to him: ‘*...ghosts of a couple of patients from the asylum...*’ He laughed out loud; it was his just his mind playing tricks. Rachel wasn’t there and she didn’t want him to join her. He waited for what seemed an age, calling her name two or three times more but still without response. Well, at least I tried, he thought. He smiled to himself, relief etched on his face that ‘*it wasn’t his time yet*’, but also slightly disappointed that his wife hadn’t bothered to show up. After all, he’d travelled well over 200 miles to be there! Oh well, he thought, she always was slightly disorganised. He laughed out loud with more gusto than he’d done in a long time. As he made his way back to his parents’ house, the smile barely seemed to leave his face. He felt contented — it was mission accomplished. He had taken on and conquered his demons.

9

Old Haunts

Andrew's plans for the week in Canford not only included an exorcism of the evil that had attacked his mind in the dream; it also provided him with a chance to experience the environment of part of his life before he knew Rachel. So many people had told him that he would never be able to go back to the person he was before he met her, but he had continually questioned that philosophy. After all, he had been happy then, hadn't he, so, why not again? Unfortunately, by the Friday, he hadn't really felt much of that happiness, surrounded, as he was, by his parents — the parents, if truth be told, he'd always wanted to get away from as an eighteen-year-old bound for university. Perhaps a return to his roots was not the answer he was looking for. The alternative that sprung to mind was to go back to Norfolk, where he'd spent the seven years after leaving school before he and Rachel set up home in Shropshire. Part of that time was before Rachel as well. Was that the solution to his deep uncertainty about the future? By Saturday, he had formalised a change of plan; he would pay a surprise visit to Rachel's parents in Middleton — just for the day. It wasn't much out of his way back to the West Midlands. At breakfast that morning, he made no mention of his plans to his own parents, but just before he left, his mother took him aside, having made sure, it seemed, that his dad was out of the way upstairs in the bathroom. She hugged him and said quietly,

"I've got something to tell you, Andrew."

He released himself from her grip and looked deep into her eyes.

"What, Mum?"

"It's you father; he's not been too well. We didn't tell you because we didn't want to burden you after your annus horribilis."

"What's wrong, Mum?"

"It's his heart, dear, I'm afraid. He had a mild heart attack back in June and was in Ipswich General for a couple of days while they did tests. He wasn't really up on his feet and walking properly until the end of July, and now he can't do anything near as much as he used to."

Andrew saw the odd tear appear in his mother's eyes. He had suspected something was wrong as his father seemed to be much quieter than usual, often taking a nap at various times during the day.

"Why didn't you tell me?"

Andrew's mother put on a brave smile.

"I just couldn't dear; not after Rachel …."

She paused and looked a little guilty.

"You're not angry with me, are you?"

"Of course not, Mum, and you're right, I probably wouldn't have coped very well with the news. How bad is it?"

"Oh, who knows, Andy? Doctor Rankin says as long as he takes it careful and sticks to the strict diet he's been given, he may have years yet."

"And if he doesn't?"

"He could find he has another attack and …."

"And that could be fatal?"

"Yes, I suppose so. Doctor Rankin wasn't too specific and I had to read between the lines."

"I'll go upstairs and talk to him."

His mother grabbed his sleeve.

"No, Andrew, you mustn't. He doesn't know I've told you — he didn't want you to know. I'll tell him sometime after you've gone back."

"Are you sure, Mum?"

"Positive, dear. Now give your old mum a kiss and be on your way — I know you'll want to be back among all your friends."

Forty minutes later, he had joined the A140 for the run up to Norwich via Diss, most of the way thinking how he'd wished he'd been able to tell his mother that his friends back in Shropshire were the last people he wanted to see right then. It was going to be hard enough to see Arthur and Dorothy Bateman, but he had to go back and sample some of his old Norfolk haunts — was there contentment to be found there?

Rather than take the by-pass round Norwich, Andrew decided to stop for an hour in the city — he and Rachel had often spent a Saturday afternoon there when they had been courting. It would also give him a chance to buy a nice bunch of flowers for his mother-in-law. Was she still that now, he wondered?

The city was busy with shoppers hunting for bargains in the sales, even though it was still only eleven. Andrew's immediate observation was how much Norwich seemed to have changed in the years since he had left Norfolk. Much of the city centre was pedestrianised and once familiar streets had become one-way. It took him a frustrating quarter of an hour to find a parking space near the castle and an equal amount of time to find a decent flower shop. Being winter, he had a limited choice of blooms so, in the end, he had to settle for a nice colourful indoor plant. At least the ceramic pot it came in looked worth the money.

The memories came flooding back to Andrew as he strolled down Middleton's High Street just after midday. Having parked opposite the bakers, Andrew first strolled towards his old flat. As he did so, he suddenly became quite nervous in case he should be recognised by anyone — a former pupil, or a neighbour, maybe? But it had been seventeen years so he quickly reassured himself that such a meeting was extremely unlikely. His physical appearance had changed so much — he was two or three stone heavier and his face had aged years in the last nine months.

The Edwardian terrace was still there and, unlike him, it appeared to have changed little in the intervening years. As soon as he'd driven into Middleton, he had immediately felt an acute sense of disappointment at how little nostalgia he felt, even given the many memories that had surfaced. Standing outside the house in which he had lived for nearly four years, that sense was heightened and sharpened. It was just an ordinary terraced house like thousands of others up and down the country. This old haunt no longer held any sentimental memories for him, and he was beginning to regret his excursion back to Norfolk. Perhaps it was true what people had said — you just can't go back to find a previous life or, at least, if you do, you won't necessarily find contentment there. He sighed inwardly and turned back for the High Street — he'd already seen enough of Middleton. It had been another bad idea and he was not going to make it worse. In any case, he could do with a nice pot plant to brighten up the lounge at *Rose Cottage*. He thanked God that he hadn't phoned Arthur and Dorothy beforehand. There would be other times when he would see them. Besides, he thought, he had chosen a stupid time and day to visit anyway — both would be busy in the shop till well after four.

He felt no regrets as he drove out of Middleton on the A1067, hardly thinking of the best route back to Shropshire. It was 12.30 p.m. and there was just one last place he wanted to revisit. With any luck, there would be some afternoon entertainment ahead — he needed cheering up and that place of relaxation and pleasure lay less than ten miles away.

10

Loosening the Chains

As soon as he drove into the centre of the small market town of Fakenham, he knew he was in luck. He could tell by the Christmas holiday crowd, which was moving in the general direction of the racecourse, that his afternoon's entertainment was guaranteed. He immediately took it as an omen that there should be a race meeting on that day. He tried to calculate the chances of it happening and with less than a dozen meetings per year, he worked out that it was about 20/1, given that there were few fixtures in the summer months at the all-jumping track.

He only just made it for the first race scheduled for the off at 1.05 — a maiden hurdle over two and half miles. According to the boards, the favourite was a horse called *Gunship*, priced at 6/4; odds which were far too short for him, particularly given that he had less than a hundred pounds on him. He'd already decided that he was going to bet small that day — £10 to win or £5 each way per race. That way, he would have enough money to last to the end of the six-race card. The aim that day was two or three hours enjoyment and not to make huge sums of money. The challenge was to break even after the six races, thus providing him with a free afternoon's entertainment.

"*They're at the start — two minutes to the off.*"

The on-course commentator's voice boomed from the loud speakers. Andrew broke into a trot. He hadn't had a chance to buy a programme so he looked quickly up and down the first board he came to in front of the grandstand. Horse number one was called *Remembrance Day*, priced at a tempting 6/1 — the day was full of omens. However, he managed to exercise caution as he addressed the bookmaker.

"£5 each way on number one, please."

"Yes, sir, that's a fiver each way on *Remembrance Day*."

Andrew handed over a ten-pound note and took his computerised slip — £46 for the win and £11 if just second or third in the 10-runner race. He had a good chance, therefore, of a profit.

The writing was on the wall for Andrew's selection almost from the start, as the maiden filly first refused to come into line and then gave a good ten lengths way to the other runners before getting into some sort of stride. Worse was to follow, as *Remembrance Day* flattened the first hurdle, thus surrendering another couple of lengths and, with its confidence gone, the horse then dived at the second, crashing to the ground with Jason Mcguire thrown forward over her head. Fortunately, both horse and rider got quickly to their feet. Mcguire's pride was shattered but not his bones. Andrew screwed up his betting slip and threw it to the ground in disgust. Like his day so far, it had not been a good one for remembrance, he thought, as he sought to insert some humour into his loss with the terrible play on words.

He was to fare no better over the next three races, losing another £30 in the process. At least, he observed, he had stuck rigidly to his plan of £10 a race. He could have tried to double up and been without money with several races to go. Like most racecourses, there were no cash facilities at Fakenham for him to replenish his wallet. So far, he had tried to carry on with the idea that the day was full of omens and had selected horses with that in mind, *Loss Adjustor* being his last pick. For the 3.05 race, he decided it was time to study form — surely he must do better. The race was an eight-runner handicap chase over three miles and the betting seemed to be wide open with the favourite at 3/1. Though it appeared to have a good chance, Andrew eventually opted for a horse named *Walk Away* priced at 5/1. He debated for a few minutes whether he should back it to win or each way, deciding in the end to opt once again for safety, splitting his £10 between win and place. Unlike the first race, *Walk Away* strode immediately into a three or four length lead, maintaining it throughout the first circuit. With less than half a mile to go on the second circuit, Andrew's horse started to pull clear, its light weight telling in the soft ground. It went on to win by nearly 20 lengths, thus netting Andrew £41.25. He had nearly redressed his balance.

It wasn't until a good ten minutes after he had collected his winnings that Andrew put some significance to the name *Walk Away*. Perhaps when he got back to Market Camton and Castlemount Grammar, that is exactly what he should do, he mused. However, after a moment's further reflection, he decided that his situation hadn't got quite that desperate yet. Nevertheless he would, at least, go and see the Head immediately on his return to school in January to request a drop down to being part-time.

By the end of the final two races, Andrew had managed to more or less break even, having covered his entry fee and some sausage and chips eaten out of a plastic tray and washed down with a passable cup of tea. The drive home was reasonably smooth, once he had found the A14 just south of Huntingdon which he had reached via Kings Lynn and Wisbech. He arrived back in Market Camton a little after eight, exhausted but in a the following in bold red ink rather more positive attitude than when he had left eight days previously. Before retiring to bed that night, he wrote the following note on his new calendar and in his 2008 school diary for the date Thursday, January 3rd:

GO AND SEE JD AT 8.30

ASK TO GO PART-TIME A.S.A.P.

NO COMPROMISE!

All three lines were in block capitals using his best red marking pen, the last line being there to remind him of his response should the Head make an attempt, as he would, to try to get him to change his mind. He had given no thought to the question he had asked himself previously and he would still have to find an answer to it, but at that moment, he actually didn't really care what he would do with the additional spare time. He just knew that he didn't want to teach anything other than A-level, and that that change had to take place as soon as it was humanly possible.

Andrew found the door slightly ajar when he arrived outside Mr Dexter's office early on the first day of term. He had decided to try to see the Head at eight, before the daily routine of assemblies took over. He'd spent an anxious few days since formalising his decision by putting his intentions down in writing. New Year's Eve had been a particularly difficult time, it being the first one that he'd been on his own for such a long time. In fact, thinking back, he couldn't even seem to recall one when he hadn't been surrounded by friends or family. He had turned down an invitation from Kevin and Sally with some firmness — they still didn't seem to understand and he suspected that they had taken some offence at his perceived rejection.

He knocked gently on the half-open door.

"Come!" bawled the Head. He sounded put out by the interruption. Andrew hesitated before he pushed on the door and walked into the 'inner sanctum'.

"Ah, Andy, come in — have you managed to survive Christmas?"

At least JD seemed sympathetic, thought Andrew.

"Well, I suppose so — in the circumstances."

"Yes, I know; Eileen and I were thinking of you. I nearly rang you to see if you wanted to join us for Christmas Day, but Eileen said you'd probably rather be on your own, eh?"

"She's a wise lady, John."

"Well, what can I do you for?"

This was the moment he'd been dreading and he'd rehearsed his answer carefully. He had intended to just come out and say it, but he started to prevaricate.

"Er, I've been having problems with 10 set 4."

"Haven't we all — I took some of them for Geography at the end of term when DC was away and they were awful."

"My 11 set 3 aren't much better," added Andrew.

"Really? Joan assured me that they were quite a nice group."

So, had he been checking up on him? What had his number two said — and why had he gone to her first? He thought of the words written on his calendar back at *Rose Cottage*. He wasn't going to compromise or have his concerns considered as some part of a general malaise in Years 10 and 11.

"I'm sorry, Headmaster, I've just had enough of the two groups."

He paused and then continued.

"And I honestly can't cope with them."

"Oh, I see — well I suppose that's quite understandable, Andrew, especially after your loss. Lost your confidence?"

You patronising, uncaring sod, thought Andrew.

"Well, what's the solution, Andy?"

"I want to go part-time as soon as possible."

Mr Dexter eased himself back in his large leather chair and locked his hands behind his head. He compressed his lips in thought.

"Not possible, right now, I'm afraid. I haven't got any spare staffing — you should know that from your knowledge of this year's timetable. Maybe from the end of this term it'll be O.K."

The Head stood up and came to sit on the edge of his desk close to Andrew.

"Unless …."

"Unless what, JD?"

"Unless your departmental colleagues can absorb the extra ten periods into their timetables."

Andrew shook his head.

"Maths is taught in sets, JD. We all teach Years 10 and 11 simultaneously."

"Yes, of course you do — how stupid of me."

JD stood up again and added,

"Can your students not be absorbed into the other sets?"

"Not unless you want groups of forty."

"Hmm, bad idea," replied JD. "Can we not remove the one or two disruptive pupils and you carry on with the rest at least until the end of the spring term?"

'*No compromise*,' he thought again.

"It's not just the disruptive ones, JD."

"Oh? They can't all be bad, can they?"

Finally, Andrew thought, I'll have to say it.

"No, of course not."

He paused.

"It's not the pupils."

Again, he hesitated.

"What then?"

"It's me."

"How do you mean?"

"I mean that *I* can't cope with teaching any more."

"Including the sixth form? I've heard no negative comments about your ability to teach them. You're one of our best A-level tutors."

"It's different with them — they seem to understand, and I can relax with them as adults. With 10 and 11, I just feel they're all against me. They're just not mature enough to understand what I've been through. You know as well as I do that if they spot a weakness in one of us then they go for the jugular and try to give us hell every lesson."

"Hmm, you may be right there, Andy."

Just as the Head had finished his sentence, the first warning bell for registration sounded. JD said,

"Well, we'll have to carry on our chat later, Andrew, but I'm pleased you came to see me, and believe me, I do understand. Let me give it some thought and I'll see what I can do. Come back and see me at the end of next week. As I said earlier, we can almost certainly arrange for you to go part-time from the end of this term. In the meantime, I'll ask Colin to keep an eye on the two groups, and, Andy?"

"Yes."

"At any sign of bad behaviour, you send the miscreants directly to me or Colin, O.K?"

"Yes, JD."

With that, the busy routine of the day took over, and over the next few days, Andrew once more found himself entangled with trying to discipline his years 10 and 11. However, having shared his problems with the Head, and subsequently with his Deputy, he was able to feel a little more relaxed and somewhat detached from his dealings with them. He was determined not to let the two groups get him down and, given he could see some light at the end of the tunnel, he reached Friday of the following week reasonably unscathed. Unfortunately, at the end of the day, when he went to see the Head for a second time, JD didn't have anything new to tell him. The situation could not be changed until the end of term, he told Andrew, when he was putting plans into action to cover his two GCSE groups from the start of the summer term, with him only having to teach sixth form from September as well. He would, of course, step down from being Head of Maths from April when Mrs Hanson would become acting head of department until the post could be advertised for September. In all likelihood, JD said, Joan's temporary appointment would be made permanent then. Finally, JD hoped that Andrew would not feel it beneath him to take on board all the help that was being offered him with regard to the discipline of his two GCSE sets. For his part, Andrew felt that a huge burden had been lifted from his shoulders, but he also noted that the Head did not there and then proffer any thanks for the seventeen years of loyal service he had given as Head of Maths, both to him and the previous Head. It left him wondering whether JD was really concerned for his peace of mind or whether he actually harboured some acrimony against him for wanting to step down from his senior position at Castlemount.

11
A Brief Affair

Surprisingly, the spring term seemed to pass quickly for Andrew with Joan Hanson appearing happier than she had done for some time. By all accounts, her divorce had been a tortuous affair, the decree absolute having come through just before Rachel died. Her children, Freddie and Sophie had been particularly attached to their father and she had found it difficult to explain to them that she and their dad just could not live together any longer. At the time, Freddie had been seven and Sophie four. However, Andrew suspected that her recent settled and contented state of mind had more to do with her impending promotion than her freedom from her former spouse.

Andrew had been dreading the first anniversary of Rachel's passing — on March the 20th — and with exactly a week to go, he seemed to be in need of some company as he lingered longer than usual in the staffroom after school that Thursday evening. Joan Hanson was the only other member of staff remaining when Andrew suddenly asked,

"Haven't you got to pick your children up from school, Joan?"

"No, their father is doing that today — he's having them for a long weekend."

"They're missing school tomorrow then?"

"St Jude's Primary has a staff training day so it seemed like a good idea, with him able to take time off more or less when he wants to."

"So, what will you do without them?" asked Andrew.

""'Oh, I don't know yet — any suggestions?"

The question had seemed innocent enough, but Andrew could swear that he detected a coy smile on Joan's face as she posed it. In recent weeks, he'd noticed the same cheeky smile when the odd innuendo had been bandied around the staffroom. Was she flirting with him now?

"I should go out and enjoy yourself, Joan. I bet you haven't had the chance to do that in a while."

"And you should too, Andy."

His heart was beating faster now. Was this leading to a date? As she leaned forward in her chair, her body language seemed to say so. He took a tentative step forward.

"Oh, I don't know — it's not much fun going out on your own, Joan."

"Why go on your own?"

"Well who else have I got to go with?"

This was definitely a two-way flirting session now. Her smile broadened, and she leant forward still further, revealing her ample cleavage.

"You don't have to look very far, Andy, you know."

"You mean …?"

"Why not?"

"Are you asking me out then, Joan?"

"Oh, I would never be so bold as to do that, Andy, but if you were to, erm …."

What had he got to lose? She was an attractive woman — a few years younger than him too. He'd never ever dreamed he would ask another woman the question that he was trying to frame in his mind. In the end, he said,

"So, Mrs Hanson, do you fancy going out with me for a drink and a meal, maybe?"

"Thank you, I would be delighted Mr Grey."

"Saturday night?" suggested Andrew.

"I'll have to consult my diary, Mr Grey — and let you know tomorrow."

"Oh, if you've got something else on, perhaps another time, then"

"Oh, Andy, I'm kidding! I don't have a social life, you idiot. My diary is totally empty. I would be delighted to go out with you Saturday evening. Where had you in mind?"

"I hadn't — it's all a bit …."

"Of a shock, Andy?"

"No, I meant a bit quick. I need to think."

"Well," Joan replied, "I would love to go out for a meal at a nice country pub somewhere, though definitely not in Camton Magna."

"Or anywhere near — the kids would have a field day," added Andrew.

"I leave the choice entirely up to you, kind sir. I can be ready from about seven — if you want to pick me up from my place. I assume you are going to drive. I've never been in sports car before."

With that, Joan stood up and bent over Andrew to plant a kiss on his cheek. Before he could say a word, and to spare his blushes, she waltzed out of the staffroom with a,

"See you tomorrow, Andy."

He sat back in his chair. Suddenly life felt good — very good. Surely Rachel would approve; she'd always got on with Joan. Besides, it was nearly a year and it was only for mutual enjoyment. It wasn't serious, was it? Also, he knew exactly where he would take her — he'd remembered seeing some nice meals being served there.

He was nervous all day on Saturday and he really couldn't think why. It wasn't as if it was a romantic date; it was just an evening out with a friend and colleague, who had had a troubled year like him. Often, when he'd heard of recently divorced couples he felt that they actually had a harder cross to bear than him. After all, he could have done nothing about Rachel's departing, while divorcees would always have some regrets or some feelings of guilt, and worse, their spouse was still on the planet to haunt and sometimes annoy them. Yes, he'd had the guilt trips, but he knew deep down he was just being self-indulgent whenever he gave into them. He had begun to recognise they were all part of the grieving process.

By five that afternoon, he'd tried on at least four different outfits, doing his best to look casual but smart, without showing he had taken too much effort. He wanted the evening out to seem to be a natural thing for two close, unattached colleagues to do. In the end, he opted for sweater and cords with a light anorak for the coolness of the early spring evening.

Joan lived on the far side of Camton Magna from his village; not far off the main road that would eventually lead them to his chosen destination. Though he'd been to her house several times before, he still managed to take a wrong turning on her suburban estate of mostly semi-detached properties. Doubling back, he realised he was then a few minutes late and cursed himself for not being so organised. He'd wanted to be the perfect gentleman for the evening, in every respect.

She was already waiting for him on her front drive when he arrived — was she nervous too? But there was something more that caused Andrew to take a second look as he got out of the car to escort her round to the passenger side. Seeing his prolonged stare, she said,

"I am dressed alright, aren't I?"

"What? Oh yes, you look stunning, Joan. I hardly recognised you — I just wish I'd dressed as smart to match."

As she sat beside him in the 350Z, the low-slung seat enabled him to study the outfit she'd chosen — a tight-fitting pale green skirt and cream blouse with short jacket to match, accompanied by gold earrings and necklace. But it was the dark green high-heeled shoes and super-fine nylons that made his heart miss a beat. He felt so under-dressed, he found himself saying,

"I feel so scruffy and under-dressed, Joan."

"Nonsense," she said, patting his left knee. "You look nice — the perfect escort. Now drive on, chauffeur."

Despite her reassurance, he still felt ill at ease. But, at least, he thought, the sweater and cords are new and he'd polished his best brown shoes as well. As he rejoined the A458 and turned the heating up a notch, he could smell her perfume as it was wafted around the Nissan's interior. Thank God, he thought, it wasn't one that Rachel had ever used.

"It's called *J'adore*, if your interested, Andy."

Had he made it that obvious that he had sensed it?

"Oh," he said nonchalantly, "it's nice."

"Thank you, Mr Grey; I try to please. Now where are you taking me?"

"You'll see — it's about forty minutes from here."

"That far? You're certainly making sure we're not seen by anyone we know."

"I've booked a table in the restaurant for 8.30 so we can have a drink at the bar first. I trust that meets your approval, Mrs Hanson?"

"Of course."

"It's not too late for you to eat, I meant."

"No, relax, it'll be fine, Andy."

Again she patted his knee, almost causing him to exert too much pressure on the accelerator and send them way over the speed limit.

The Dog and Pheasant was quite crowded when they arrived, and though Andrew managed to find them a couple of seats in the lounge bar, it took him over five minutes to get some drinks — half of Guinness for him and a brandy and coke for his partner for the evening. On his return from queuing at the bar, Joan asked,

"This looks a nice pub, Andy — how did you find it?"

"Er, oh I was just out for a drive one day last summer and just happened on it," he lied confidently. He couldn't tell her what had happened the first time he'd been there. At least, not yet anyway, he thought.

"So you never brought …?"

Andrew read her thoughts.

"No, I never brought Rachel here."

Joan smiled; she looked a little relieved.

"Was that bothering you, Joan?"

"I'm not sure — maybe. I don't know, Andy, it must be difficult for you."

"In what way?"

"Well, going to certain places that might hold memories for you."

"Maybe in the early weeks, but not so much now."

He paused to take a gulp of beer.

"At first, I found it hard even to go to the same shops to buy food without her, you know."

"That's understandable — I had the same kind of problem after Nick left. You get a feeling that it isn't quite right, don't you?"

"Yeah, I suppose so. In my case it was coupled with feelings of guilt."

"How?"

"I felt guilty because I was still alive and able to do all the things that we used to do together. But …."

"But?"

"But, I think in some ways it's much harder for you because Nick is still alive. I don't have Rachel to haunt me."

"Nick doesn't haunt me, Andy."

"No?"

"Not really."

She paused before going on.

"I suppose I have to think about him sometimes, especially when he's having the kids. I guess you could call that being haunted. Really, I just get angry and frustrated."

"Frustrated that things might have been different and that you and Nick might have stayed together?"

"Definitely not, Andy. At least not as far as we were concerned — maybe for Freddie and Sophie it might have been better. Did you and Rachel miss having children?"

"To begin with, yes, but when we knew we couldn't, we adjusted our lives accordingly. I think, in some ways, it made us closer as a couple. We'd both had to accept we weren't going to raise a family, and we didn't then have any distractions."

"Kids aren't distractions, Andy."

"No, I didn't mean it like that. I meant that it threw us together more without children being the centre of the marriage — *we* were the centre."

"I see."

By the look on her face, Joan seemed to be about to dig deeper into his past when suddenly a student-looking waiter carrying a couple of menus appeared beside them.

“Sir, Madam, you’re table will be ready in five minutes. Perhaps you would like to look at the menus before you come through.”

Andrew took them and passed one to Joan. He felt somewhat relieved that their discussion had been interrupted. It had brought back too many memories. He would try to steer the conversation away from his and Rachel’s life together.

If he hadn’t noticed them when they’d first arrived at the pub, he certainly couldn’t miss them when they stood up to go into the restaurant. Drawn either by Joan’s outfit or by her tall statuesque figure, crowned with her long blond hair, several heads again turned to gaze in their direction. His pride was heightened still further when, as they walked through the bar, she pushed her left arm gently under his right. He hadn’t experienced a warm sensation inside like that since Rachel had first held his hand when they went shopping in Norwich for the very first time.

Over dinner, Andrew managed to keep their conversation on either school matters or about his guest and her two children, with Joan content to chat at length about Freddie and Sophie. It was obvious that she loved them dearly and that they were the centre of her life. The meal was every bit as good as Andrew had hoped it would be — Joan seemed to have a healthy appetite and at the end of the evening over coffee, she reached her hand across the table to hold his. He felt a tingle run up and down is spine.

“Andy, that was a fabulous meal — thank you so much for inviting me out.”

“My pleasure entirely — we must do this again sometime.”

“Yes, we must, Mr Grey.”

The formal use of the name she often used for him at school gave Andrew a hint that, despite their evening out together, they should and must not forget their professional relationship when they returned there on Monday. Later, as he dropped Joan at her house in Camton Magna, any thoughts that Andrew might have had about taking the evening to another, more intimate level were quickly quashed. Having walked her to her front door, she turned to him and said,

"I won't ask you in for a coffee, Andy. I hope you understand."

"Of course, Joan — thank you for a lovely evening."

"No, thank *you*, Andy."

As she uttered her words of gratitude, she bent forward and gently kissed his cheek, and before he could say a word, she had opened her front door and disappeared from sight, leaving a faint waft of *J'adore* behind her in the cold night air.

March the 27th came and went surprisingly comfortably for Andrew. Despite waiting nervously for the telephone to ring, he was somewhat relieved when it didn't. He would have found it difficult to pick up the receiver anyway, let alone have an unemotional conversation with anyone, which would have probably led to a night of misery as his loss came back to haunt him. He reassured himself that friends and family were probably as nervous as he was about communicating on that day of all days. Joan did send a text message which read simply,

'Thinking of U.'

She and Andrew were to repeat their night out on a couple more occasions during April, both on weekends when her husband had Freddie and Sophie. On the first such occasion, the evening finished in much the same way as previously with Andrew feeling slightly disappointed that it hadn't concluded in a more intimate way. However, on the second evening — the Saturday before they were due back to school on the Monday for the summer term — with Joan seemingly about to kiss him goodbye, she said quietly,

“Do you fancy a coffee, Andy?”

Andrew was silent for a few seconds while he put the inevitable interpretation on her question.

“Oh, that would be nice, Joan — thanks, I do.”

“Good.”

Once inside her house, she did manage to put the percolator on but neither of them drank any coffee as Andrew quickly took Joan in his arms in the kitchen. She did not resist, and five minutes later they were ‘trying’ to make passionate love in the bedroom, both suffering both from an apparent over-eagerness and a complete lack of practice in such an intimate engagement. Afterwards, as they lay side by side, both of them tried to express their embarrassment at what had just taken place between them. Andrew went first.

“I’m sorry, Joan, I didn’t want it to happen like that. It’s been such a long time. I was hopeless.”

“It’s O.K, Andy, you were fine. You seem to have forgotten that it’s been longer for me — much longer.”

“How long?”

“Over two years. Nick and I slept in separate beds well before he left.”

“Well, I just hope you don’t feel bad of me.”

“Don’t be silly, Andy. We both needed it and it gave me back my self-respect to think that I was still wanted.”

“Me too, I suppose.”

“You sound as though you have regrets.”

“No, it’s not that — I don’t have any doubts on that score and, Joan….”

“What?”

“It was fantastic.”

"Thank you, kind sir."

She paused and rolled over to look at him.

"So why did you say, '*I suppose.*'

"I was just thinking about Rachel."

"Andy, she would want you to be happy and enjoy yourself, you know that."

"Yeah, I …."

"Don't say it, otherwise I shall begin to doubt whether you actually did enjoy it."

"Sorry."

"Don't be; it must be hard to engage in intimacy after you lose someone you love so dearly. But surely life is here to be enjoyed — Rachel would want that, wouldn't she?"

"Yeah, I …."

"Andy!"

"Yeah, you are right."

"That's better. No regrets, then?"

"No, none."

He was in need of a drink when he got back to *Rose Cottage* on the first Monday after school, and it wasn't because of any problems he'd had with his remaining sixth form groups that day. His part-time status had been confirmed right at the very end of the previous term with a supply teacher engaged to take his Years 10 and 11. No, he was happy and content with his reduced timetable, able to teach in the area where his expertise and confidence were best suited. There had been a different problem that he'd had to face on the first day of term — and it had scared him. Whether by accident or design, the truth of the matter was that several colleagues at school seemed to be aware of his and Joan's new 'relationship', with Kevin, for one, making one or two pointed comments during the day. When Andrew had been in the staffroom at break and lunchtime, Joan had done her level best to sit next to him and in as intimate a way as possible, without actually sitting on his lap. Several colleagues who had clearly witnessed her 'over-friendly' behaviour gave Andrew knowing nods and winks afterwards. This was precisely what he hadn't wanted. It could lead to professional problems, especially if the pupils found out. It just wasn't on; surely she could see that, thought Andrew as he sat down in his lounge with a large tumbler of whisky. Yes, they were both unattached, but a school was too close an environment for such open and outwards signs of affection between two members of staff. Most pupils were not mature enough to handle such a liaison sensibly and he could soon become the butt of typical schoolboy humour, even despite the sympathy that still abounded for him with most of the students. Apart from some cheese and biscuits in a vain attempt to soak up the alcohol, he drank most of a bottle of whisky that evening, collapsing into bed well before ten — drunk, and his mind in a whirl as to what he should and must do about Joan's public displays of affection.

They were sitting in her lounge with Freddie and Sophie playing upstairs on the computer. He felt nervous and unsure of himself. Things had moved so fast he'd hardly had to time to think and take stock of his situation. Joan emerged from the kitchen carrying a notepad and pen. Andrew knew what she was going to say.

"Well, we'd better make a start at a wedding guest list, Andy, love."

"Really, it's still over six months till the day."

“Yes, dear, but these things take time to organise; people book holidays at this time of the year and I want everyone to reserve the date now.”

“O.K.,” he replied somewhat reluctantly.

“Oh come on, Andy, you sound as though you’re not that keen to get started on it.”

“No, I am, but ….”

“There’s a ‘but’? You’re not having second thoughts about it, are you?”

“No, of course not.”

“*Yes, he is*.”

The voice came from the direction of the stairs which led down directly into Joan’s lounge.

“Sophie, have you been listening, you naughty girl?”

But Andrew knew it wasn’t Joan’s daughter’s voice.

“Sophie, come down here this minute!”

Joan was angry now.

“*He doesn’t want to marry you; he doesn’t love you*.”

Joan got up and headed for the bottom of the stairs.

Andrew cowered in his chair — he’d suddenly guessed what was happening to them.

“You come down here now, you little madam,” she screamed at the top of her voice. The noise echoed round the walls of the small semi. Andrew put his hands over his ears. The voice continued, nearer now.

“*He doesn’t love you because he still loves me*.”

“What on earth are …?”

Joan stood rooted to the spot a few feet from the stairs. She was looking up them with terror written all over her face.

"Oh my God, Andy!" she screamed louder than the first time. "Do something!"

Slowly, Andrew got to his feet and moved over to where Joan was standing, by which time the origin of the unknown voice had become apparent to both of them.

"Oh for goodness sake, Rachel," he sighed. "Please go away."

Rachel calmly walked down the remaining few stairs and sat down in the chair Andrew had just vacated. Joan continued to stay where she was, fixed to the floor like a block of ice.

"No, Rachel, that's enough," said Andrew, his voice louder now.

"*I'm not going anywhere until you promise me you won't marry that.*"

She was dressed casually in clothes he didn't recognise. He moved forward to touch her. She screamed.

"*Promise me! Promise me*!"

By this time, Joan had collapsed into a heap on the lounge carpet, sobbing uncontrollably.

"Wha-what's happening, Andy?"

It was his worst nightmare — how had she found out about Joan and him?

"*Promise me! Promise me*!"

Rachel screamed again. He knew what he must do — he'd known all along. He tried to say the words but his lips seemed glued together.

"*Promise me, or you'll have to join me*!"

Now she was threatening him. He tried again to part his lips. A mumbled response eventually came out.

"I-I promise."

"*Say it again, and this time mean it*!"

"I promise, I promise, I promise."

He kept on shouting his pledge. The room had suddenly become pitch-black and shrouded in silence, broken only by his heavy breathing as he continued to swear his oath. He was sweating profusely but his body felt ice cold.

"Rachel!" he screamed. "I do promise you!"

Suddenly, some light returned and, as his eyes opened, the realisation hit him. It had all been a dream; a nightmare where reality had seemed to mix with the downright terror of his wife's phantom appearance. He sat up and turned on the bedside table lamp. He looked at his alarm clock — it was 4.30 and it was Tuesday morning. The previous day's events came back to him and he shuddered at the thought of where his 'affair' — if that's what it could be called — might lead. He gritted his teeth, and though there was no one there to hear him, he said in a determined voice,

"I will see Joan today and finish it. I do not love her; I will not ever love her like I loved Rachel."

With his mind made up he fell quickly back into a dreamless sleep waking just before seven, surprisingly sober given the amount of alcohol he'd drunk the previous evening. He was still in as determined a mood as he had been a couple of hours earlier.

12

Unwelcome News

To ensure complete privacy and avoid any public displays of emotion, Andrew pushed a memo into Joan's pigeon hole first thing on Tuesday morning. He kept its contents as bland and as professional as possible. Even though he was no longer head of department, he hadn't yet really come to terms with the consequent demotion and it read much like such a note would have done had he still been Joan's line manager. It said,

Need to see you on a departmental matter
after school in my room. Thanks.
AJG

Though she didn't show as much open affection during the day as she had done the previous day, Joan still continued to wink occasionally at Andrew, accompanied each time by remarks such as, '*A private audience, Mr Grey*?' and '*Am I teacher's pet, Andy*?' Andy did his best not to show any emotion at these quips, merely nodding blandly in the professional manner he had often used with members of the department when serious educational matters needed to be discussed.

Though there was the familiar gentle tap on his door just after the end of school that afternoon, Joan did not wait to be called in. As Andrew got to his feet from behind his desk, she rushed across the room and flung her arms around his neck, kissing him freely on the lips. She stood back and said,

"God, I've waited all day to do that!"

"Joan!" he said firmly. "Someone might come in."

"Who cares? A lot of people know something is going on, Andy."

"Do they, Joan? And how has that happened?"

"I don't know," she replied weakly.

"Well I do, Joan, now please sit down. I want to talk to you."

"Ooh, you are masterful, Andy!"

Realising finally that her ex head of department was in a serious frame of mind with a departmental issue to discuss, she flounced into his one easy chair and retorted,

"O.K., O.K, what's the big deal? And why do I have to see you in your room? I'm your boss now," she said with a meaningful grin.

"Sure you are — at school," he replied with equal meaning. "I just didn't want us to be disturbed, and if I'd come to your room we might have been. It's less likely here now I'm just a poor part-timer."

"You're choice."

She seemed a little irritated now.

"Thank you for that, Joan."

"Sorry, I didn't mean anything by it."

By this time, he had returned to the safety of his chair behind the barrier of his desk. Joan leaned forward in her chair.

"Well, what is it, then?"

"Joan, I've been thinking."

"You're regretting your decision to drop down to part-time?"

"No, it's nothing to do with school — well, not really."

Joan did not reply — she seemed to suspect what was coming.

"Joan," he started. Joan's face took on a serious expression. In a quiet voice, Andrew continued,

"I don't think we should see each other outside of school anymore."

"Oh, why ever not?"

"Because I don't want to."

She looked torn between a sarcastic reply and floods of tears. It was a facial expression he'd never seen before on a woman's face. '*Beware a woman scorned*' rang in his head. There was an awkward silence for a few seconds until, with sarcasm gaining the upper hand, Joan managed to say,

"So you didn't enjoy our nights out together or sleeping with me?"

"Of course I did, Joan."

"Well why am I being dumped, then?"

"You're not."

"Sounds like it to me, Andy."

"You would only be being dumped if we had a boyfriend/girlfriend relationship in the first place."

"Well, didn't we have?"

"I didn't think we'd reached that stage, Joan. I enjoyed your company and the dinners out and the sex was fantastic, but …."

"Yes?"

"Well, for one thing it's too soon for me. I'm too vulnerable."

"So you do have regrets — I just knew it."

"Not regrets, Joan."

"Well what, then?"

"I just made a mistake and I realise it's not what I wanted right now. I hope you can understand that."

"So you wish you'd never gone to bed with me?"

"I don't know, Joan. I just think it was too early and the wrong time for me. And don't get me wrong, I still want us to be friends, and besides, we have to try and be professional at school, don't we?"

Joan's face darkened — he'd never seen such an evil look before.

"Sounds to me as if I've been used to help your social life — enable you to have some nice meals without being on your own. It sounds like I was only a paid escort."

"I'm sorry you feel like that, Joan. I'm just trying to be honest with you and tell you how I feel. And I hoped we both enjoyed the meals, not just me."

Joan stood up. It was clear she was desperately trying to keep hold of her emotions before she broke down in tears.

"So, is that all you wanted to see me about?"

Andrew got to his feet.

"I'm so sorry, Joan — still friends?"

"Maybe — we'll have to see, won't we?"

And then she was gone, the door slamming behind her, leaving Andrew wondering whether he'd actually made the situation far worse. There was no doubt that his new head of department had been scorned and he knew that, if she had a mind to, she could make his life in school more difficult than just her over-affectionate behaviour of the last two days had done. Despite this worry, he couldn't help but feel that an enormous weight had been lifted from his shoulders.

For the remainder of the week, Andrew was fortunately able to avoid Joan with relative ease. Only being in school on Mondays, Tuesdays and Thursdays meant that he managed to get to his first ever long weekend unscathed by any embarrassing or awkward moments. In addition, on Thursday, he took the opportunity to wander into the centre of Camton Magna during his several free periods, thus further avoiding having to see his new head of department. On the odd occasion when their eyes met in the staffroom or the corridor, she quickly averted her eyes and turned away from him. Wednesday was spent largely trying to tidy up the garden at *Rose Cottage* accompanied by a few hours relaxing in a deckchair catching up on some reading. However, the second week of term turned out neither as ordered nor as pleasant, when on the Tuesday just after school had finished for the day, Joan came to see him in his room. She did not bother to knock and, without ceremony or comment, she placed a folded piece of A4 paper on his desk directly in front of him. She did not wait for him to pick it up and read it, but quickly flounced out of the room without saying a word. He waited for a few moments before looking at the mysteriously delivered piece of paper. It was her proposed staffing for the coming academic year. All was as expected until he looked at the last line. Directly below his sixth form teaching, it read:

11 set 4 Mathematics JSH (3) + AJG (2)

He could not believe his eyes. She was proposing that he should take a double period of Year 11 Maths with the very set that had caused him so many problems that year — the same set who had been the main reason for him wanting to go part-time and teach only in sixth form. Not only that, he was going to share that group with her. So, was this the start of the outpouring of her scorn? He was immediately filled with an almost uncontrollable anger and his heart began to beat faster. She just couldn't do this to him. Clutching the staffing sheet in his hand, he jumped from his chair and was outside her room in a matter of seconds. Throwing open the door, he shouted,

"What the hell is this, Joan? Are you having a joke?"

"I'm sorry, Andrew, is there a problem?"

She spoke calmly and with some arrogance.

"You're damn right there's a problem. I specifically asked not to teach any group outside the sixth form."

"Can't do it, I'm afraid. I'm on an afternoon course for most of next year and my Year 11 group needs covering. You were the only member of staff qualified and available to take them. And please don't shout at me, Andrew."

It was obvious from her manner that she had thought carefully about how she was going to discuss the departmental staffing with him, as she had remained calm and in perfect control of her emotions during her response to his outburst.

"Well, we'll see what JD says about it, shall we?"

"I don't think you'll have much joy there — I've already seen him, and I think you'll find that your contract does not prohibit the odd period of GCSE teaching, especially when there is no other solution. Remember, Andrew, you are part-time now and can no longer pick and choose your classes. Also, it hasn't gone unnoticed by other members of the department that you are likely to have such an easy timetable next year.

"Easy? They think teaching A-level is easy?"

"It is for you. Besides, it's only two periods out of eighteen, for goodness sake. I'll be setting and marking most of the work and your time will be spent largely getting them to work through past papers, given they take GCSE next June. I am trying to do my best for you, Andrew."

"Well, all I can say is you've wasted no time in working out the staffing, Joan. I didn't used to start until half-term. We've been back less than two weeks this term."

"I started thinking about it as soon as I knew I would be acting head of department. Can you blame me?"

"That means you were already thinking about this when we were …."

"Let's keep this professional, please, Andrew. Now, if you don't mind, I need to go and pick the children up, so unless there's anything else…."

"Not for now, Joan, but I *will* go and see the head tomorrow."

"I'm afraid you won't, Andrew."

"What do you mean?"

A sarcastic smile filled her face.

"You're not in tomorrow. Remember, you're only part-time."

In the end, Andrew didn't go and complain to JD. When he got home that Tuesday afternoon, he dug out his new contract, and to his dismay, he discovered Joan was right. All it indicated was that '*where possible*' he would only teach A-level, but that '*he would have to be available to take GCSE classes, should the need arise in exceptional circumstances.*' She had obviously convinced the head that her course was an exceptional circumstance.

After a few days, he had managed to put the matter more or less behind him. After all, he kept telling himself, next year was nearly four months away. Apart from this hiccup to his new routine, the remaining weeks up to half-term followed a similar pattern as the first had done, with Andrew also able to attend one or two midweek race meetings at Wolverhampton to help occupy his time. He found himself settling into a routine he could handle for just about the first time since Rachel had died. That routine was to be shattered on the last Friday in May at the start of his half term break.

It had not been a very successful afternoon. Four races gone, with his wallet lighter by over two hundred pounds, and his trip to Dunstall Park was beginning to seem like a bad idea for the first day after an emotionally draining half-term. He needed a result in either of the last two races, and according to his programme, both fields were likely to be headed by a low priced favourite. He didn't have enough cash left to back anything less than about 5/1 if he was to make up his losses. He needed a tip from somewhere, or someone. Suddenly, as he strolled towards the bookies' boards, a vaguely familiar voice whispered in his ear.

"Alroit, mate?"

He immediately recognised the Black Country tone.

"Yeah," he replied, glancing sideways at the man responsible for his previous successful tip. "Could do with another tip like the last one, though."

"Yeah, we made a bit on that one, didn't we? How much did yow put on?"

"Oh, just a tenner," he lied.

"I had a score each way and made a pretty packet. The winnings kept me going for weeks, mate."

They had reached the line of boards now and Andrew sighed audibly.

"What's up, mate?"

"It's not worth betting in the next race; the favourite's four to one on."

"Nah, I'm waiting for the five past five race."

"Got another tip, then?" asked Andrew cautiously.

"Maybe."

"Gonna' let me know?"

"Maybe."

Andrew began to understand.

"What's it gonna' cost me?"

"A foiver, mate."

"And if it loses?"

"I'll give yow your money back — can't say fairer than that."

"Deal," said Andrew.

"Money first."

He handed over the money and said,

"The favourite looks like it'll be about evens."

"Yeah, but number seven is your horse — *Robin de Creuse*. It's handicapped to go well."

"Likely odds?" asked Andrew.

"Ten or twelve to one."

"Win or each way?"

"That's up to yow, mate. It depends how lucky yow feel."

"If the rest of the afternoon is anything to go by, not very."

"Put your bet on with *Honest Dave* and I'll meet you in front if his board after the race, O.K?"

"Sure."

Suddenly, Andrew felt a vibration in his left-hand trouser pocket — his mobile phone was ringing. Who on earth could be trying to contact him? Few people now phoned his mobile — only Joan had done so in the last few months, and though his parents and brother had the number, he couldn't remember the last time they'd used it. He took it out and looked at the screen; it was his mother phoning from her mobile. His heart starting thumping and he nervously pressed the green button.

"Mum, how are you?"

"Andrew, I've got some bad news, dear."

His mother's voice quavered; she seemed on the verge of dissolving into tears.

"What, Mum?"

"It's you father, Andrew; he's been rushed into hospital in Norwich."

Andrew was trembling now.

"Oh no," was all he could manage.

“It’s his heart, dear; another attack, the paramedics said. He’s in intensive care now — the doctors haven’t told meanything yet. I’m so afraid, Andrew.”

His mother started to sob.

“P-please come quickly, Andrew.”

“I’ll come straightaway.”

“Thank God, please hurry.”

“I’ll be there as soon as I can, Mum.”

“Thank you, lo….”

Her voice tailed off and the crying got louder. She was obviously overcome with emotion and it had taken all her strength and resolve to phone him. Though she tried to say more, Andrew didn’t understand another word. He pressed the red button and looked at his watch — it was four-thirty. His mind was in a whirl and he had to make a decision about the last race, due off in thirty-five minutes. His heart was telling him he should drop everything and run to his car for the drive to Norfolk; his head was telling him otherwise. Being already at Wolverhampton, he was at least forty minutes closer to Norwich than if he’d been at home. He made his decision — his head won. He was surprised at how calm and pragmatic he’d been in his decision. In any case, he’d kind of been expecting such news. A little part of him, however, knew he was doing wrong, but Rachel’s death had sparked a change in him that had only just surfaced with his mother’s phone call. Though he didn’t realise it there and then, he had become hardened to tragedy and other people’s misfortune or sorrow.

13

More Guilt

The 'tip' came in last, trailing the winning favourite by twenty lengths, but Andrew didn't stop to see the end of the race, let alone meet the Black Country stranger to return his five pounds. The writing had been on the wall for *Robin de Creuse* after about two furlongs. He could still hear the racecourse commentator lauding the winner's success as he climbed into his car in the car park behind the grandstand.

The journey took him exactly three hours as he broke several speed limits in his anxiety to make up for the time he had wasted, which by his calculation was about forty minutes. He didn't even bother to get a parking ticket at the Norwich and Norfolk University Hospital on arrival at just after a quarter past eight — a decision he would regret later when he would receive notification of a forty-pound fine. The intensive care unit was on the ninth floor and he was in front of the reception desk within five minutes of parking his car.

"Yes, sir, who are you looking for?"

"Mr Grey, please."

The female receptionist looked at a chart in front of her.

"Are you a family member, sir?"

"Yes, I'm his son — please hurry."

"Oh, I see."

She seemed hesitant and unsure as to what to say next. She looked up at Andrew and did her best to force a smile onto her face.

"Well, I think you'd better go down to the last room on the left at the end of that corridor behind you. I think your mother is there with one of the nurses."

"Thank you."

Andrew turned and tried not to break into a run. As he got to the room the receptionist had indicated, the door opened and a pretty nurse emerged, almost colliding with him.

"Oh, I'm sorry, sir — you must be Andrew."

"Yes, that's right — is my mother in there?"

"She is, sir."

The petite, dark-haired nurse put a hand on his arm and added,

"And I'm so sorry, Mr …."

Andrew didn't wait for her to finish; the word 'sorry' had been enough for him as he brushed past her into the small private room. His mother was seated looking out of the window and staring at the twilight sky. She looked round on her son's entry.

"Oh, Andrew, he's gone, dear."

She struggled to her feet and clasped him to her.

"When, Mum?"

"Oh, only about half an hour ago — you've just missed him."

Andrew held his mother away from him and gently kissed her wrinkled forehead.

"I'm sorry, Mum, I did my best to get here as quick as I could."

It was only a white lie, wasn't it? He just couldn't tell her the truth, but he knew he was already filled with guilt — guilt born out of his own stupid selfishness. Later, he would realise that those feelings of guilt had other origins, based in the past and going back to his childhood. Even then, as he sat down beside his mother and gently held her hand, he was hit with the sad realisation that he had never ever said that he loved him. His mother broke his thoughts.

"I'm going to miss him so much, Andrew. I just don't know what I'm going to do."

"It's alright, Mum, I'll come and stay with you for as long as you need me."

"But your work, dear, you have to get back, don't you?"

"Not for over a week; it's half-term till the 2nd of June."

"Then there's the funeral to arrange, Andrew. I'm not sure I can …."

"I'll sort that, Mum, please don't worry."

"And I haven't had a chance to phone New Zealand — they'll only just be waking up, I think."

Andrew put his arm round his mother.

"Mum, I'll phone Tony when we get back to your place. Is there anything left you've got to do here?"

"No, that nurse was going to fetch me a cup of tea, but I'm ready to go home now, dear. I think I have to get a certificate or something."

"Later, Mum, I'll do that later. Let's get you home. Did you drive here?"

"No, I came in the ambulance."

"Well, just you wait here for a couple of minutes while I go and see the receptionist and then we'll be off."

His mother nodded.

"I'm so glad you're here, Andy. I just don't know what I would have done without you."

He could feel the tears welling up inside him, and they weren't only tears of sadness — they were also heavily filled with the guilt that came from lying to his mother at such a tragic time. He felt awful — almost worse than when Rachel had died. Somehow, he had managed, through his own selfishness, to taint his father's death.

With so much to organise and so many people to meet, including relations from all over the country, Andrew had little time to himself over the next few days. He had to steel himself to the thought of another funeral, and in his few free moments, memories of the corresponding week after Rachel's death came flooding back to haunt and fill him with remorse once again. Two people who he'd loved dearly had gone and he had survived. Though he knew that death was random, or at least out of human hands, he was still dragged down again by guilt that he was still alive.

It had taken until Monday to get the funeral organised — a simple burial at the local Anglican church in Canford on the Thursday afternoon. Tony, his brother, had earlier phoned to say that he wouldn't be able to make it, causing his mother to break down once more. Andrew did his best to comfort her and also remind her that actually Tony and his father had never really got on with each other. Most of the time, when Tony had lived in England, they had shown open antagonism to each other born out of a mutual disrespect. It was going to be hard enough for everybody without having that past of their past raked up.

At first, Andrew managed the ordeal reasonably well, especially with a few whiskies to give him some much needed Dutch courage. But ever since he had known the date and time, he had been dreading the event, with so many memories of Rachel's to cope with. It got worse for him during the ceremony, when the vicar mentioned the family's previous recent loss of his wife and his parents' daughter-in-law. On the verge of tears to begin with, the vicar's words were the straw that broke the camel's back and Andrew collapsed in uncontrollable sobs. His mother was to put her arm round him for virtually the rest of the service. He just about managed to stand upright in line after the funeral to greet and shake hands with the mourners, though he was able to say little on his mother's behalf by way of thanks for their condolences.

By the evening, with his mother's favourite sister — but his least favourite aunt — going to stay with his mother for a week or more, Andrew felt that his responsibilities were more or less over, especially as his Aunty Muriel seemed to want to contradict everything he said or did with regard to his mother's future care and healing after her loss. He was in two minds as to whether to return to Shropshire that very evening, but in the end he gritted his teeth and opted for leaving early the following morning, giving him a full weekend to get organised before going back to school for the last half-term of the year. At least, that is what he told his mother and aunt when, in reality, he hoped that he would have little teaching for some weeks, as his Year 13 groups were on permanent study leave and his two Year 12 groups would also be away on exams for four or five weeks.

Over the next few weeks, Andrew found himself being used more and more as cover for absent colleagues. At first, it had come as a bit of a shock to him, even though he knew he should have realised that being part-time, and therefore paid by the hour, the Head was duty bound to ensure that his timetable was kept as full as possible. Consequently, on most days, he would be unaware until he got to school what classes he would be 'baby-minding', as several colleagues were prone to call cover periods. Previous problems he'd had with the two GCSE Maths groups began to surface again as, like most part-time teachers, he found that the pupils did offer his as much respect as if he'd been full-time. To their naïve way of thinking, part-time teachers were part-time because they did not want to give as much commitment to their work, including not giving them as much help and care as they might.

Somehow, he managed to survive till the end of term, but it took many evenings spent recovering with alcoholic pick-me-ups to do so, both at *Rose Cottage* and at various pubs of his choice. He became less and less fussy about such choices, often frequenting the *The Royal Oak* in Market Camton, particularly as it was within walking/stumbling distance of home. In addition, but not entirely to his liking, he and Kevin would often go for a drink there on a Thursday evening after one of Sally's meals. He found the conversation with Kevin continued, as always, to be centred on school or his favourite football team and whenever Andrew tried to talk about the present state of his own life, his friend seemed disinterested or incapable of offering much advice other than to continually question why he had found the need to go part-time. As far as Andrew was concerned, Kevin and Sally just did not understand. At times, he felt that they didn't even *try* to understand, preferring instead to think that everything should stay exactly as it has been when Rachel had been alive, even down to suggestions as to how Andrew kept the garden at *Rose Cottage*. Despite this, Andrew still kept going out with Kevin, but it was more out of respect for Rachel's friendship with Sally rather than any personal desire to keep the arrangement going. The only plus point, as Andrew saw it, was that it gave structure to one evening during the week at least. Needless to say, when the August holidays arrived, Andrew was ready for a complete break from school as well as friends and colleagues with well-meaning intentions. His other 'problem', namely the relationship with his head of department, had become much less of a worry. She seemed to have taken a fancy to one of the young English staff who was about ten years her junior. However, the occasional smirk she gave him when they passed in a corridor said more about her attempt to 'get even' with him than with any intention to start a long-lasting and meaningful relationship with the young teacher.

Though he had been looking forward to the holidays, when they actually arrived at the end of July, he again experienced the same emptiness he had felt exactly a year before. Yes, for one reason or another, he had found school tough, but at least it had provided some kind of structure to his week. Now, for six and a half weeks, he had no such structure — only feelings of guilt over Rachel's and his father's deaths. He had no one to share the holidays with and no one really he could share his innermost feelings with either. In short, he just could not see where his life was going — it was sliding out of control, dictated by his emotions and inability to cope with the recurring depression that weighed heavily down on his body and soul.

14

Breaking the Chains

If he didn't know at the start of August what he needed to do about the direction in which his life was heading, then he certainly knew he couldn't avoid addressing that question by the last week of that month. The dog days of August were always traditionally a time of apprehension for Andrew as the impending new school year loomed before him. New classes to teach always caused some anxiety, even for the most experienced of teachers. Like an actor, performing a role on stage for the very first time, there was always that nagging doubt that he would not be liked, or even appreciated, therefore causing him problems as a result.

He had done his best to enjoy himself during the holidays, desperately trying to ease up on the drinking and gambling which seemed to have crept up on him and become such a regular part of his life. Despite his drop in salary, he was still very comfortably off with no mortgage and only the car loan to finance from his monthly outgoings. On the good days, where he avoided both of his vices, he found he could live surprisingly cheaply, especially by shopping round for the bargains in the supermarket. It actually gave him some pleasure to see how little he needed to spend in order to live. He'd never been one for buying clothes, and since Rachel's death, he'd taken much less pride in his appearance anyway. Holidays away from *Rose Cottage* had begun to seem pointless now that he had no one to share them with — Rachel had been the one who had adored the Spanish sun, not him. He was content to sit in the garden with a good book, or a crossword, and a can of ice-cold lager.

During the last weekend of the holidays, with far less preparation of lessons than normal to do, and to ease the tension he felt at the prospect of the new term, he decided to sit down with pen and paper on the Sunday afternoon to reconsider his financial circumstances in some detail. Without really being aware of it, something in the back of his mind was nagging him into thinking about the possibility of being able to resign from Castlemount Grammar and leave teaching for good. Truth be told, he had thought of the possibility, but had always dismissed the idea, being afraid of what people would think of him. But, over the previous eighteen months, he had become less and less concerned for his public persona and more concerned with his own inner well-being.

Apart from the regular utility bills, his only other fixed commitment was the car loan, of which about £6,000 remained outstanding. The Nissan 350Z was still worth at least £16,000, so it would be paid off if he sold it. He could replace it with a cheap run-around for a couple of grand. At the end an hour of mental arithmetic, he had come to the surprising conclusion that, if he didn't have a job, he could still survive where he was for up to a year, living off the proceeds from the sale of his sports car. Surely he could find something else to do in that time? And if not, he could always sell the cottage and buy a flat. After all, he didn't really need a three-bed cottage. That was again paying homage to his public image. The sale of the £200,000 property would give him enough money to buy a decent apartment and provide him with a good living for a very long time indeed.

By the time he had returned to school the following day, he had almost convinced himself that he was in a position to hand in his resignation, with Christmas being a real possibility. Even if he only kept the plan on the back burner, it had vastly improved his inner well-being, knowing, at last, he was in charge of his own destiny. In any case, the financial assessment he'd carried out had given him renewed confidence for the immediate future, and any apprehension at teaching new groups seemed to have waned somewhat. Even the prospect of having to teach his old 10 set 4 in Year 11 appeared no longer to be at the forefront of his mind as it had been when he'd first learned a double period with them was on his timetable.

In the end, September turned out better than Andrew had expected, both because the weather was warm and also because his students appeared initially docile and ready to get back into the habits of study and learning after the long summer break. Once again, he had an extended weekend with Monday and Friday being his days off. For almost the first time since his wife had died, he felt reasonably content with his routine, seeking to fill his free time with long walks in the country, drives to places he hadn't visited before and the occasional visit to Wolverhampton or Uttoxeter for race meetings. Of course, there was the inevitable marking and preparation of lessons. His drinking still continued but nowhere near as heavy or as desperate as it had been. He felt, at last, that he was beginning a new chapter in his life. That was until a major crisis stopped him his tracks during the first week in October.

His Year 12 lower A/S set had hardly said a word to him over the first four weeks of term — it had taken all his guile to get them to respond to him in class. He had taken very few of them lower down the school but had heard from other members of the department that they were likely to be a very weak set in the sixth form. The previous week he had set them a staging test in order to see what they had learnt and, more importantly, what they had retained. He was to be horrified with the results. Taking a reasonable pass mark at 30%, no less than twelve of the fifteen students had failed to achieve that score with five even in single figures. With the top mark still less than 50, Andrew could never remember having such a disastrous set of results in the whole of his previous teaching career. He was not best pleased when he took them for the first time after the test. The group looked nervous as he stood in front of them waving their test papers in the air. He did not mince his words.

"These are by far the worst tests at A/S I have ever seen at this level."

There was a mumbled response from one of the students on the back row.

"What was that, Jayne?"

"She said, whose fault is that, Sir?" said Tom Peters.

"And what does that mean, Jayne?"

Jayne Coldwell didn't murmur this time but said loudly,

"It means, Sir, that we don't understand you, so it's your fault and not ours that we can't do the Maths."

"Really, Jayne? And have you tried? Have you ever told me that you can't do it? Have you ever come to me for help?"

Jayne said nothing. Tom came back.

"It's not just Jayne, Sir; we're all finding it difficult."

Andrew felt himself getting warm; his heart was beating faster. He tried to remain calm.

"I see," he said quietly. "Well, we'll have to do something about it, I think."

Not knowing what he meant, any murmuring stopped as they all fixed their eyes on their teacher.

"First," he continued, "I shall go through every single question on the board until you have a complete set of solutions for the test. Then, next week, you will sit exactly the same test again, without your notes, and if anyone fails to achieve a mark of, let's say, forty, then I shall recommend that they drop A/S Maths."

The silence continued until Jayne Coldwell broke it with,

"I can't see the point in that, Sir, when I won't understand what I'm writing down anyway."

"We have to start somewhere, Jayne, and I'd be grateful to you if you would be a little more positive in your attitude, please."

"What's the point, you …."

Jayne Coldwell didn't finish her sentence. He couldn't be sure, and he certainly didn't want to find out by pressing her for it, but he suspected that she had been about to say, '*you can't teach*,' or something similar.

All but one of the students achieved the required pass the following week, including Jayne Coldwell. In the end, Andrew didn't recommend that that student drop the subject. With all the negotiations with parents and, of course, his head of department, he just couldn't face the hassle or confrontation involved. Unfortunately, despite this apparent success, the A/S students remained somewhat uncooperative and antagonistic towards him, so much so that after another couple of weeks, he found himself dreading taking them almost as much as he had dreaded taking his 10 set 4 the previous year. Worse was to come when, at the very same time, that very set began their disruptive behaviour again. By the last Monday of the month, he had reached a much more critical and desperate position than when he had first decided to go part-time. As he sat in his lounge late that afternoon, with the light fading fast after cold, wind-swept and wet day, his future in teaching looked as dark and as bleak as the weather outside. He just couldn't go on — he'd begun to lose his students' respect. Some had never given him any since he had gone part-time. In one brief cry of desperation, he looked up at the ceiling and howled.

"Oh God, please help me!"

And then he wept uncontrollably, banging his fists on the arms of his chair in frustration. After what seemed an age, he got up and fetched a pad of paper from his desk. The outburst had concentrated his mind as to what he must do. He felt calm and could wait no longer. No one was going to make him change his mind. He opened the pad and started writing.

Rose Cottage,
Church Lane,
Market Camton,
October 27th 2008

John,
I write this with a heavy heart and I will try to keep it brief. You must have known that I have never had the same confidence to teach as I had before my beloved wife passed away. Going part-time was the first step to try to help me with this. That step has failed and I no longer can face teaching any longer. Consequently, I shall not be returning to Castlemount Grammar to teach. I know I am letting you and my colleagues down in making this decision and, I suppose, my students too. However, I think that if I continued I would be doing them a great disservice as I don't feel able to give them the education they deserve. In short, I have totally lost my confidence to teach.

I would be grateful if you do not press me to change my mind over this matter and that people will leave me in peace. Of course, I realise that I am breaking my contract and though I am not certain of the legal position, I would not expect to be paid from the end of the current month. I trust you will soon be able to cover my teaching commitment. I wish you and all my colleagues well and every success for the future as I formally resign my post as part-time teacher of Mathematics.

Sincerely,
Andrew Grey

Given that he knew he couldn't get the letter to school for the Head to be able to read it first thing in the morning, there was only one course of action open to him. Gritting his teeth, he donned an anorak for protection against the rain and set off for number 17 Church Lane.

At first, standing outside the Simpson's cottage, he was going to put the letter addressed to Mr Dexter through the letterbox in the hope that Kevin would take it in with him in the morning, but then he decided that he had to make certain that he would do that the very minute he got to school. He pressed the bell. A few seconds later, Sally opened the door.

"Andy, good to see you. Come on in out of the rain."

"No, I won't, Sally, if you don't mind. Is Kevin in?"

"He's not Andy, I'm afraid — he's gone to do some shopping for me. Is everything alright?"

Despite the dim light, Andrew could see the concern etched on her face. He had to get this over quickly.

"Would you give this letter to him, please, and tell him to give it to the Head as soon as he gets to school in the morning."

"Of course, I will, Andy — now what's this all about? Why can't you do it? I thought you taught on Tuesdays."

"I can't tell you right now Sally — just ask Kev to get the letter to the Head first thing in the morning."

"O.K., but are you sure …?"

Andrew didn't reply as he'd already turned his back on her and was walking down the front path.

The phone rang five times that evening, causing Andrew eventually to take it off its hook. He only answered the first call which came just ten minutes after he'd got back to *Rose Cottage*. By the end of it, he'd learnt his lesson. The call was inevitably from Kevin Simpson who immediately expressed his concern.

"Hello, mate, what's wrong? Are you ill?"

"Er, no not really, Kev; I just want you to take the letter to JD for me, please."

"Yes, of course I will, but if you're not sick why aren't you going in?"

"Please, Kevin, I'd rather you didn't ask. Just let the Head read the letter. I expect he'll tell you afterwards."

"Hmm, sounds mysterious, mate. Can't you tell me, old friend?"

Andrew wiped the tears from his eyes and replied as best he could.

"No, I said I'd rather not. Now if you don't mind I'm going to hang up."

He didn't wait for or listen to any response and carefully replaced the phone in its cradle. Though he didn't answer the phone again that evening, he recognised the Head's number when it came up on the LCD screen, making Andrew suspect that Kevin had phoned him not long after his difficult conversation with him. Judging by the other calls, the Castlemount grapevine had clearly swung into action with some speed. As he went to bed that night, surprisingly without any alcoholic aid, he just hoped that colleagues would leave him alone after the Head had read the request for privacy

15

A Burden Lifted

He was up very early the following morning, determined not to be at *Rose Cottage* should anyone, particularly Kevin or Sally, decide to come round to find out what was going on. Though he had tried to make it clear in his letter that he didn't want anybody trying to make him change his mind, he knew that one or two people would still probably ignore that plea, purely out of a genuine concern for his well-being. At six-thirty that morning, his well-being hadn't been better for a very long time — a huge burden had suddenly been lifted off his back and his life had taken on a whole new meaning. As he gazed out of his kitchen window, mug of coffee in hand, he heard a lone blackbird singing its nonsensical tune from a bush in the back garden. He smiled with pleasure. He hadn't listened to a sound like that in ages and it felt good to be alive. He leant across the sink and opened the window, breathing in all those garden smells that he seemed to have forgotten. All at once it hit him that it was actually a privilege to be alive and not a heavy yoke that had weighed him down almost beyond what he could bear. To be able to see and hear all the natural things that God had designed for man had suddenly taken on an importance and necessity for his sanity. Since Rachel's death, he had been too busy with his own self-pity to notice that there was a world outside the self-indulgent workings of his mind. His put his half-empty mug down on the kitchen worktop and stretched his arms to their fullest extent. Life was indeed very good.

He took just enough clothes for two or three days. He had no idea where he was going to go, except that it had to be well away from Market Camton and Castlemount Grammar School. He was as free as a bird to do exactly as he pleased; even though he knew he would now have to instigate his ‘plan for survival’, as he called it. Top of the agenda in this plan was liquidating his car — a visit to a couple of garages in Camton Magna at the weekend should take care of that. In any case, his bank balance was healthy enough for a few weeks living expenses, and that was assuming his salary stopped from the end of the month. The Head might even be able to persuade the governors to pay him until the end of the year. After the dedicated service he had given to the school, that was perhaps the least they could agree to. As he drove north and west on the M6, he frankly didn’t care — at that moment, it was enough for him just to be free from the responsibilities that had been on the point of giving him a complete breakdown. Some might say that he’d already had a small one without really knowing it.

Unlike the previous day, the weather was fine and sunny with little breeze to speak of. Though it was nearly November, it was pleasantly warm, again in complete contrast to the previous day, when the weather had been so much in cahoots with his mood. Though he didn’t really need reassurance that he had been right to do what he had done, the sudden change in the weather seemed, at least, to be in total agreement with that outrageous decision.

Reaching Junction 15 after about an hour of driving, Andrew felt in need of some fresh country air. The day was too good to miss to be sitting in the closeted comfort of his 350Z, and with an earlier than usual sunset later due to the change in the clocks, he was anxious to make the most of the late October sunshine. If he was open to any omens that day, another one presented itself to him as he took the exit from the motorway where the sign read: *Market Drayton 15 miles*. The name was close enough to that of his own village to be a pointer as somewhere to stretch his legs. In the end, it didn’t really matter where he went that day — he was simply enjoying the new-found freedom to make as many random choices as he liked.

Parking his car in the centre of the small North Shropshire market town, Andrew immediately had feelings of déjà vu as he strolled past the small antique and gift shops. The only explanation he could come up with for this feeling of familiarity with his surroundings was that he and Rachel must have visited the town not long after they moved from Norfolk; probably on one of their initial explorations of their new county. The mediaeval covered market hall, in particular, brought back memories of sheltering from an April shower as Rachel moved from one quaint shop to another. Did he buy her that brown leather handbag from one of them? Twenty-four hours earlier, he would have probably wept at those memories of happier times — now he felt entirely different about them. Now they gave him a lift and an apt reminder that death cannot take away or erase special shared memories. He may not have Rachel any longer but he would always have those. The sun was warm on his face as he approached the *River Tern* with its inviting towpath for a nice long walk before lunch at *The Tudor House* in the square. His whole being was glowing with happiness and a contentment that he'd been without for so long. He was on one of those 'highs' and at that moment he didn't ever want to come down from it.

As he joined the towpath heading upstream, he glanced at his watch — it was five to eleven. With about two hours remaining before lunch, he decided to walk for about an hour and then either walk back the way he'd come, or cross over one of the many footbridges to return by the other bank. He soon dismissed the latter option when, after about half a mile, he could plainly see that there were no further footbridges as the river narrowed and led into open countryside. Indeed, given he wasn't wearing any decent walking boots he even had to dismiss his first option as well and return to his starting point by the way he'd come after only about thirty minute's walking. After such a good start to the day and his new life, he was slightly annoyed with the forced change of plan, leaving him somewhat flat after the one or two omens that seemed to have presented themselves to him. As he saw it, he had three choices: continue his walk downstream; return to his car and drive somewhere else or take an early lunch. He selected the third option.

As it name implied, *The Tudor House* was an oak-framed building dating back to Elizabethan times and which was now Market Drayton's premier inn for good food, wine and ale. Despite the lack of exercise, Andrew had acquired a satisfactory thirst and he headed for the public bar to spend some time reviewing the previous eighteen hours over a pint of the local brew.

As he took his first gulp of the appropriately named 'Shropshire Lad', he began to reflect on the enormity of what he'd done. By then, everyone at Castlemount Grammar School — except maybe the pupils — would know of his desertion from his post. What would they be thinking of him? Who would have tried to phone him? He'd deliberately left his mobile at home to avoid even having to think about answering any calls. He just didn't want anyone trying to get him to rethink his decision, or worse, tell him he should see a doctor and get signed off sick for a few weeks. That would only prolong the agony — it had to be a clean break without the medical professionals getting involved to complicate matters. Of course, people would think him daft not to try and obtain six month's sick leave on full pay, followed by six months on half. But, money wasn't an issue, provided he could sell his car, and that should be easy given the popularity of the Nissan 350Z. In any case, what if his doctor denied him sick pay? In that case, he might have had several months of hassle and worry when in fact as far as he was concerned there was nothing to worry about. The main thing was that he was now free — free from everything that related to his former job and colleagues. It didn't really bother him that, for one reason or another, he had been particularly close to two of them — Kevin and Joan. In the case of the latter, his new situation was a vast improvement on having to suffer her stares or sarcastic grins and comments. Kevin was more of a worry or, at least, Sally was, given her mother-hen type nature. He thought he could manage Kevin alright and, if the worse came to the worse, he could always put the second part of his master plan into operation and move into a flat somewhere else. By the time he had finished his pint, such a move had moved nearer to the front of his mind.

"Having a late break, friend?"

The accent was definitely not local. Andrew turned to face the speaker who had joined him at the bar.

"Just a day out, mate," he replied.

"Lucky you; nice day for it as well. Fancy another?"

"That's very kind of you — I'll have a pint of Shropshire lad, please."

"No problem — I'm Paul by the way."

"Nice to meet you, Paul, and it's Andy."

"Two pints of the Lad, please, love."

The girl behind the bar smiled and took the men's empty glasses. Andy felt relaxed in the company of the stranger.

"You don't sound local, Paul."

"No, I'm from Kent originally — born and bred in Herne Bay."

"What brought you up this way?"

"Work, really — and we couldn't afford to get on the housing ladder down south."

"Married, then?"

"Divorced — she's taken the kids and gone back to be near her parents in Whitstable."

"What do you do, Paul?"

"Electrician, and luckily, I'm done for the day. What do you do that allows you to take a day off midweek?"

"It's a long story."

The drinks arrived and Paul said,

"I'm a good listener."

Then, Andrew spent a good ten minutes explaining his personal circumstances, going right back to Rachel's death and ending with his walk-out from school. When he had finished his monologue, interrupted only by the occasional 'really?' or 'good for you' from Paul, Andrew felt uplifted that he had, for the first time, been able to relate the previous eighteen months in its entirety to someone, albeit a complete stranger. It made him feel good that at least one person, other than himself, was now fully acquainted with what had really happened to him. None of his friends, colleagues or family could say that. All they had was an assortment of pieces of an incomplete jigsaw on which they had each put their own individual, and mostly wrong, interpretation. It had taken a chance meeting with a total stranger for Andrew to put all the relevant facts together at one time. Later, he would regret not having recorded his story.

"Quite a tale, Andy," said Paul, when he'd finished.

"In some ways, I don't suppose it's any different or more unusual than what happens to thousands of people everyday all round the world.

Except, how many people just walk out of a job without a by-your-leave, especially a teacher? I bet that doesn't happen very often."

"It did to me, Andy — twice, in fact. Well, once from a job, anyway."

"Yeah?"

"I wasn't always an electrician. Once, I was head chef at a pub much like this."

"Why did you leave?"

"Couldn't get on with the manager, so one day after another row with him, I just stormed out and never went back. Didn't even go back and pick up my things."

"Didn't he try to sue you?"

"What for? He didn't have to pay me any redundancy or severance pay. In fact, he still owes me two week's wages, truth be told."

"You said there was another thing you walked out on."

"Yeah, from the wife. Haven't seen her since. Everything was dealt with through the solicitors."

"What about your kids? Don't you see them?"

Paul took a long swig from his glass."

"No, not since I left."

"Don't you miss them?"

"What do you think, Andy?"

"I don't know; Rachel and I never had any kids, so I can't really understand what that must feel like."

"Come on, Andy, drink up; let's have another."

And they did — and one or two more as well. Any thoughts of a meal in the inn's renowned restaurant went out of the window and by mid-afternoon, Andrew was ready to get his head down somewhere. Though his new friend tried to insist that he go back with him to his flat a short walk away, Andrew had earlier made up his mind that he was going to treat himself that day and stay at a nice hotel or inn for a couple of nights. For his part, Paul wished him good luck in his new life and gave him his mobile number should he want to repeat their afternoon together if he was ever in the area again. Even though Andrew told him that he might well do that, he knew he almost certainly wouldn't. After they had shaken hands, Andrew ordered a double whisky which he downed in two gulps. He then made a rather unsteady journey through to reception where he procured himself a nice single room on a bed and breakfast basis until the Friday morning. By four that afternoon, he was fast asleep, fully clothed and lying on top of the bed.

Inevitably, when he woke just after eight in his darkened hotel room, he had come down from his 'high'. He felt slightly nauseous, and though he had thoroughly enjoyed his afternoon drinking session with Paul the electrician, his over indulgence had certainly caught up with him. An hour of drinking copious amounts of cold water out of a hotel plastic glass, which he had to fill at least a dozen times, went some way to flushing the alcohol from his system and rehydrating his body. In between the numerous gulps of water, he did manage to have a shower so that, by five past nine, he felt reasonably refreshed and crying out for food.

He was clearly the last person to arrive in the quaint dining room and, at first, Andrew felt certain he was too late to obtain a dinner. Only a couple of tables remained occupied with diners finishing their desserts or coffee, and there seemed no one about to show him to a table. Just as he was about to find his own, what looked like the senior waiter appeared from a hidden door in a side wall.

"Ah, have you recovered, sir?"

Had it been that obvious to the hotel staff that he and his Paul had drunk so much? Andrew smiled weakly and followed the waiter's directions to a table near a window.

"I bet you're hungry now, sir, aren't you?"

Andrew was now getting tetchy at the man's over-familiarity.

"Just bring me the menu, please," he replied.

"Of course, sir, right away."

He couldn't have been more patronising in his reply if he'd tried.

"I'm afraid you're too late for the beef and I hope you're not a vegetarian because that option's all gone too."

Andrew said nothing as the waiter continued.

"And what would you like to drink, sir?"

"Just water, please."

The replied had been forced out of him. He just wanted the man to go away and bring him a menu. The waiter continued to be condescending.

"Of course, sir, just what you need, I suspect."

"The menu, please waiter!"

Andrew's reply was loud enough for one of the remaining diners to raise their heads from their dessert and turn round to stare in Andrew's direction. At last, the waiter seemed to get the message and he moved quickly away, clearly surprised that his customary 'friendly' manner had been misinterpreted. When he brought the menu, Andrew had to answer another question — one that he'd not faced before and one that was to put a dampener on his meal that evening. It was one he would have to deal with several times again, especially when he went to stay at hotels or eat out on his own in restaurants. The waiter, at least, seemed rather humbler and genuinely concerned for Andrew.

"On you own tonight, or is your wife joining you?"

He knew what he wanted to say — the plain and simple truth that his wife was dead, but he didn't want to embarrass or further hurt the poor waiter's feelings. He was only doing his job, after all. He gave a brief and non-committal reply.

"No, I'm on my own."

The waiter seemed to sense that his polite enquiry had struck a chord with Andrew, as he then busied himself by removing the spare place setting opposite him. Suspecting he was dealing with a recent divorcee, he said,

"I'll leave you in peace and come back when you're ready to order."

Wednesday dawned sunny and Andrew awoke refreshed after a good night's rest. The awkwardness he'd felt on his own in the dining room the previous evening was not repeated at breakfast. With a buffet-style arrangement, he felt it easy and quick to satisfy his needs and be out in the sunshine without having to talk or listen to anyone, particularly the waiter who'd tried to belittle him.

That day, like the following, he spent on a mixture of driving the North Shropshire back roads and walking in the gently rolling hills. He did not take his evening meal in the hotel's dining room again, preferring instead to eat a cooked meal at lunchtime in a couple of country inns he came across. Room service satisfied his needs in the evening, and he did not venture down into the bar again, thus avoiding any further comments from the hotel staff.

When Friday morning came, he found himself torn between extending his break and returning to Market Camton in order to set about selling his car, a prospect that he wasn't looking forward to and which had been constantly on his mind since he had left on the Tuesday morning. He had had such a good time that his eventual decision to return home was made with a heavy heart and with much reluctance, but return home he did to spend the weekend visiting several garages. He knew he might not have enough time to advertise and sell it privately. He also knew that he would only get the bare minimum for it from a garage. In the end, a deal was struck with the garage he'd bought it from, the final offer being a mere £10,750 plus a five-year-old VW Golf 1.4 with nearly 50,000 on the clock. A Golf had always been in his top four or five cars, but not one as old or as timid when compared to what he had been driving. At least he was able to pay a decent cheque into his account on the following Monday, making him financially secure for a year or more.

During the weeks leading up to Christmas, he tried to occupy his time as best he could — his gambling became infrequent and then only for small stakes of a few pounds. The weather took a turn for the worse so he was unable to enjoy many walks. In short, nothing he turned his mind to helped him recapture the joy and contentment he'd felt while he'd been away from Market Camton for those three or four days at the end of October. He avoided answering the phone at all costs and, after a few vain attempts at seeing him, even Kevin and Sally gave up and left him alone. His other former colleagues seemed to have taken his request for privacy seriously as well. He'd had to take just one prolonged call from John Dexter immediately after he'd returned from North Shropshire in which he informed him that the governors had accepted his resignation but with much reluctance and some sadness. To Andrew's amazement, they had also agreed that he should receive his salary until the end of December like any teacher who resigned in the normal way at half-term.

The only person he kept in regular contact with was his mother back in Suffolk. He was heartened to learn from her that friends and neighbours had rallied round and that she seemed as happy as she might be given her sudden and tragic loss. The one thing he hadn't done was to tell her that he had given up teaching. He knew he had to do that with her face to face. He had not wanted to burden her with his own problems when her remarkable fortitude and resilience had helped lift him a little out of the depression that had returned through lack of things to occupy his time. Because of this, he knew soon he would have to think again about the second part of his master plan. After his time in Market Drayton, he just sensed he would be so much happier living in a new environment as far as possible away from Market Camton and his old life. With so much change on the horizon, let alone that which had already happened, he also made the decision early in December to spend his second Christmas without Rachel with his mother in Canford. He would tell her then of what he'd done and discuss with her his plans for the future. After all, she had known him since he was born; she knew who he once was and she would understand his desire to get back the happiness he'd had then as a boy growing up. No doubt they would shed many tears as they shared each other's grief. The mother/son bond had now taken on a new significance for them as they each faced the future as single people.

16
New Horizons

He'd toyed with the idea of parking the silver Golf around the corner from his mother's 1950's detached house on the western edge of Canford. He knew as soon as she saw the car, she'd question him as to what had happened to his lovely 350Z. In the end, however, as he approached the village from Ipswich that Christmas Eve, he decided it would save him finding the right time to tell her of his desertion from Castlemount Grammar. With the day dark and dismal, she might not come to the front door to greet him anyway, and he could slip into the house before she had a chance to observe his car on the drive. He was wrong, as his mother was standing at the open door waiting expectantly for him. He barely had a chance to get his suitcase from the boot before she rushed towards him to give him a hug.

"Oh, you've changed your car," she quickly observed. "Not as nice as the other one, dear. You'd not had it long, had you?"

"No, Mum, I hadn't. Let's get inside and I'll explain. It's cold stood out here."

"Yes, I've just made a nice hot pot of tea."

"I could do with something stronger."

"A bit early for that, Andy — still I suppose you deserve one after your long drive."

"I do, Mum."

A few minutes later, with whisky in hand, Andrew and his mother were sat in her cluttered lounge. He began slowly.

"Mum, I've been looking forward to coming back to Canford for Christmas."

"I've been looking forward too, love. Quite like old times, except for …."

She paused and looked at a photo of Andrew's father with Rachel at his side on the mantelpiece.

"Not quite, Mum, but we'll still have a good time, eh?"

"We'll try. Now what's happened to the car?"

She looked nervous.

"You didn't crash it, did you? I always thought it was too quick for you."

"No, Mum, I didn't have an accident. I had to sell it."

"Had to? Why, are you short of money?"

"Not really, but I don't have a job now."

"What on earth did you do?"

She was looking really anxious now. He quickly put her mind more at ease.

"I just quit — at the end of October. I just walked out one day."

His mother appeared relieved.

"Oh, I thought …."

Andrew didn't ask his mother what she'd thought as he said,

"I'd just had enough, Mum. I was having problems with one or two classes and I suppose I'd lost a lot of my confidence to teach."

"What will you do for money? I can lend you some. You father left me well-provided for."

"No, Mum, I have enough at least for a year, now that I don't have a mortgage. Selling the car gave me enough for that and besides, the sports car was only a kind of compensation after Rachel died."

"What will you do, love? You've always worked."

"I don't know yet — not teaching; at least not in the normal sense. I could always do some private coaching. I just need some time to sort myself out."

"What did the school say?"

"I don't know; I haven't been back. The Head phoned and wished me well and thanked me for all I'd done."

"I should think so too."

"You don't seem upset, Mum."

"Why should I be, dear? After all, it was only a job and you're health is more important than that."

"Thanks, Mum, I was dreading telling you."

"You should have told me when you quit."

"You had enough problems of your own, Mum."

"Oh, I'm alright now. I'm thinking of doing something like you've done."

"You don't work, Mum."

"No, but I'm probably going to move from her — it's too big for me now."

"It was too big when Dad was alive."

"I know, but we loved it. Now, it doesn't mean so much anymore."

"Where will you go?"

"I've looked at one or two places in Ipswich, nearer to your Aunty Muriel. I like the shops there and there's the theatre as well. I feel a bit stuck out here now I haven't got you dad to drive me. It's forty minutes on the bus into Ipswich and they only run every two hours."

"Won't you miss your friends in Canford?"

"Not really, and anyway, I would only be moving about twelve miles away."

His mother paused. She seemed a bit nervous.

“I’m having the house valued in the New Year.”

“Good for you, Mum.”

Andrew’s mother seemed a little surprised by his reaction.

“You don’t mind?”

“Why should I mind? Besides….”

He hesitated before continuing.

“Yes?”

“I’m thinking of moving too, Mum.”

“Where?”

“I have absolutely no idea yet. I just know I need to get away from Market Camton.”

“Too many memories?”

He’d forgotten how wise and perceptive his mother could be.

“Yes, I suppose so.”

“And your close friends don’t say the things you want to hear or need?”

“Yes, but ….”

“Oh, don’t worry, son, I’ve had the same feelings. My neighbours and friends here in Canford just don’t understand what it’s like — why should they, unless it has happened to them?”

Andrew suddenly felt warm inside. His mother’s astute observations had lifted him up on another ‘high’ that cold bleak Christmas Eve. He said simply,

“Thank you, Mum.”

“What for?”

“For being so wise and understanding.”

He put his whisky glass down on a side table and walked over to his mother. He bent down and kissed her lightly on the forehead.

“Above all, Mum, thank you for being you.”

And then they cried, hugging each other in mutual relief at having shared some of their grief and innermost thoughts. When Andrew eventually sat down to finish his whisky, he felt filled with joy and gladness that he had decided to come to Canford for Christmas.

And enjoy it he did, with mother and son able to reminisce and exchange further feelings about how they had both coped with their individual grief. One conversation on New Year's Eve, however, was to stand out above the rest with regard to Andrew's future. The topic that he had raised with his mother concerned his father's beginnings and childhood.

"So where exactly was Dad born, then?"

"The North East."

"Oh? I though he was born in Suffolk like you, Mum."

"No dear, it was by the sea in a place called Sandsend. He took me there once when we were first married. It's just a tiny fishing village a few miles north of Whitby, as I recall."

"Is that where Dad got his love of fishing from?"

"Oh yes, Andrew; his dad and granddad were both trawler men out of Whitby from before the war. Don't you remember when you were a boy how he always said he wanted to buy a small fishing boat to use off Canford? He used to take you out in Harry Marsden's little dinghy instead. He never got his wish, did he?"

"No, Mum, he didn't."

They both fell quiet for a few moments, until Andrew said,

"I'd like to take up fishing again, you know. I've certainly got the time now. You never know I might even make a small living out of it."

"It would please your dad, dear, especially if you got a boat. He'd look down and watch over you when you were out on the sea."

"What's Sandsend like, Mum?"

"I can't really remember; it was years ago. Whitby's nice, though, if a bit touristy in the summer. It's a different world up there, especially with their accents. All I can remember about Sandsend is the cold east wind, some red cliffs and lots of little fishermen's cottages. Not many shops; just a few tearooms and so on."

"Sounds nice."

"It's certainly a long way from Suffolk."

"Or Shropshire, Mum."

"I expect so."

And that was it as far as Andrew was concerned. He needed to hear no more as he changed the conversation to his mother's childhood.

Three days later, when the estate agents were open again after the Christmas and New Year break, Andrew Grey walked into *Culper and Denhams* in Camton Magna to place *Rose Cottage* on the market at the tempting asking price of £194,995. However, it was to be more than another month before he was able to drive north to stay at a bed and breakfast in Whitby; his adventure to look for new horizons having been delayed by the worst January weather in almost thirty years. In the mean time, despite it being about the slowest time of the year for selling houses, he still managed to accept an offer of £190,000 for his cottage in Market Camton. By the end of January, *Rose Cottage* was sold subject to contract, with Andrew agreeing to vacate the property by the end of March at the latest. So excited at his new future was he, he was prepared to move out and rent somewhere in Sandsend or Whitby if he was unable to buy somewhere in time. He had several sleepless nights and second thoughts during his waking hours about whether or not he had made the right decision, calling such occasions his 'cold moments'. Deep down, however, he knew it was what he desperately wanted, and every time it snowed again in Market Camton, he became even more anxious to get on with his new quest for freedom. His mother also managed to sell her house, putting down a deposit on a nice retirement apartment in a converted mansion on the outskirts of Ipswich, set in 40 acres of its own grounds and containing several kinds of leisure facilities for residents of advancing years. Andrew took his mother's prospective move to be another omen, giving him confidence that he was about to find new horizons too.

17

Getting it Back

He fell in love with Sandsend from the very moment he saw it for the first time. It was early February and the weather had so far been kind to him since leaving Shropshire the day before. He had spent a comfortable night in one of Whitby's many guest houses that lined the cliffs above the town. He'd been fortunate that *The Miramar* was open for business at that time of the year. Now he was finally in the location of his choice to start a new life — or indeed regain the one he'd had before he'd met Rachel. He had taken particulars for just two properties in the seaside village. There were more, but they were too big, too small or just in the wrong place. He would arrange with the agents in Whitby to see either or both of the two chosen properties later if he liked them.

Number 7 *The Strand* was the first he came to and he knew the instant he saw it that he didn't need to bother with the second, or any others for that matter. As its address implied, the narrow terraced cottage fronted the gently sloping beach across a road and ancient promenade. As Andrew parked a few doors down, he glanced at two fishermen casting their lines into the North Sea. The location was perfect. If he lived there, he would have all of a fifty yard stroll and he would be doing the same. He looked down at the sheet of particulars; the asking price was a mere £105,000. With agents, solicitors and removal fees to pay, he could still clear upwards of £75,000, thereby providing him with a small monthly income in interest. The prospect was too exciting for words, and within twenty minutes, he was back in Whitby in the offices of *Barnes and Edwards* requesting a viewing. Mr David Edwards immediately rang the vendor and an appointment was made for an hour later at eleven-thirty.

Though the vendor would be at work, the agents had keys to show Andrew round the property.

The cottage was small — just two rooms downstairs and two bedrooms and a bathroom upstairs. The kitchen and bathroom both looked newly fitted, but it was the living room on the ground floor that thrilled Andrew the most. Virtually the whole of the front wall was fitted with a double glazed window through which the views of the beach and the sea beyond were magnificent. As Andrew gazed through it, David Edwards could see the excitement on his new client's face.

"Well, what do you think, Mr Grey?"

"Magnificent, absolutely magnificent."

"Tell me, then, what's your position at the moment? Have you a property to sell."

"Yes, it's already sold subject to contract."

"Who with?"

"Oh, you wouldn't know them; they're back where I live, in Shropshire."

"Ah, I see; Jackie didn't tell me you weren't local. Moving up here for work?"

"Something like that."

"Well, the vendor is anxious to move quickly — I believe he starts a new job in York in about a month."

"Is he open to offers?" asked Andrew, still staring longingly at the sea.

"I'm not really allowed to say, Mr Grey, but the current asking price was fixed so that in the end he would hopefully get a nice round figure, if you get my meaning."

The estate agent winked at Andrew. He got his meaning.

“Tell him, I’ll give him £102,000 — that should make him happy, no?”

“I will certainly try that for you, Mr Grey. Now if you drive me back to the office we’ll sort some preliminary paperwork out — and you can give me all the details of your agents and solicitors.”

Within the hour, Andrew had more or less bought himself a delightful fishermen’s cottage in the seaside village where his father had been born over seventy years previously. So far, it all felt right and any ‘cold moments’ seemed to have kept themselves away from Andrew’s mind and soul.

That evening in his room at the guest house in Whitby, Andrew received a call on his mobile from Mr Edwards to inform him that Mr Wilson had accepted his offer of £102,000. Already, March 21st was being suggested as a possible completion date. Andrew had exactly six weeks to sort things out, not least of which was all the surplus furniture etc. he would have to sell, give away or simply take to the local tip in Camton Magna. The prospect ought to have frightened him, but it didn’t. He had made a bold start at getting his old life back.

He was absolutely ruthless in his disposal of things that he knew he’d never be able to get into his new cottage. Though he managed to sell most unwanted furniture by advertising in local papers in and around Camton Magna, the rest of his unwanted possessions were simply taken to the tip. He’d already previously got rid of all of Rachel’s clothes and many of her personal things at charity shops and the like. He kept back a few shared things that had special memories attached to them, including the brown leather handbag that he’d bought Rachel in Market Drayton all those years before. In the end, he was ready for the move in good time for the proposed date, which finally became fixed when all contracts were exchanged on March 7th.

At first, when he moved into *7 The Strand*, Andrew began to feel at home, and in the early weeks, at least, he began to experience a remarkable transformation in himself. Now, no one knew him and no one was aware of his recent tragic past. Now, he could be who he wanted to be; free of all baggage associated with Rachel, both physical and mental. He didn't have to talk to anyone if he didn't want to. As a boy, he'd always been shy and retiring, preferring his own company to that of others. It had only been Rachel that had taken him out of himself, but now she was gone, he could try to become the 'Rock' and the 'Island' of one of his favourite Simon and Garfunkel songs. He began to take up again all the solitary pursuits he'd enjoyed as a teenager back in Canford. He filled his days that spring and early summer with walking, reading, mathematical puzzles and fishing from the narrow strand opposite his new home. The move seemed to him to have been a good one; his gambling and drinking halted completely as he enjoyed his possibly temporary 'heaven on earth'. This new-found contentment with himself was, however, inevitably tempered with the occasional 'cold moment' when he began to wonder if he really had made the right decision and if he was only kidding himself that he was in heaven, but, each time, he quickly tried his best to dismiss them. Eventually, however, each time they seemed to last longer than the time before.

As summer reached its height, his contentment started to bring back the feelings of guilt again. Guilt that he was enjoying himself and Rachel wasn't. Somehow, in the back of his mind, he'd known that it would be an inevitable consequence, if he ever did find happiness again. Yes, he'd enjoyed being a boy again but thoughts of Rachel had also never been far from his mind. How could he marry the two together? How could he get his previous life back — the one he had enjoyed so much in the first few weeks in Sandsend? Was it just transitory? Had his marriage to Rachel changed him so much that there could never be the permanence in such a simple life that he thought there could be? At times, he would remember when he had left home at eighteen — how in reality he'd been desperate for a new life at university. So why was he trying to recapture the time before he left home? As summer moved into autumn he became weighed down with the awful realisation that he had been kidding himself that he could go back. Yes, he'd done it for a while, but like someone who takes up a jigsaw again as an adult often finds it more boring than they did as a child, so he was becoming equally bored with simple boyish pleasures. He simply wasn't a boy anymore so why on earth should he have thought he would enjoy being one again? All in all, it was his worst nightmare — he'd burned his bridges and he felt lost with no one around him that he could turn to. The fact that no one knew anything of his past was now turning against him in his hour of need. He didn't really know anybody in Sandsend to talk to anyway and he just couldn't bear to go back to Shropshire to see anyone. There was nobody he could turn to, he thought, that is, except for one person — a person who nine months before had shared their deepest thoughts with him about what the future held for them.

18

Paradise Regained

He could barely remember how he'd got there. The sea was rough again and the tide was right in. The light was fading fast at the end of a fruitless day filled with envy at Bordock Hall. His mother had been well — surprisingly well. It had been obvious to Andrew from the very minute he'd seen her again that her move had been a total success. As they took afternoon tea together outside on the lawns at the rear of the luxurious retirement home, he was amazed how many new friends his mother had made in the six months since she had become a resident there. Unlike him, she appeared really happy and contented in her new environment. She brimmed with excitement as she told him all about the hall and its facilities, occasionally pointing out to him people who she had got to know since they last had met. Every time he tried to interrupt her in order to share his problems with her, she seemed to dismiss them as either trivial or merely temporary with remarks like, '*Oh I'm sure you'll settle down soon*' or '*well, you'll just have to get yourself a job again*'. After a couple of hours in which she also showed him her apartment and the remainder of the hall, he felt his journey had been a waste of time. His mother was too full of herself and her new life to be bothered with or try to understand what was going on in his. When he left her just before seven that evening, he was filled with frustration and utter desperation at the futility of his lot, so much so that he knew he just could not return to Sandsend. He felt lost with his mind spinning out of control and he desperately needed to see and talk to Rachel once more.

Standing with his feet at the very edge of Canford Cliffs, he called out again and again.

"Please come back and see me, Rachel!"

When he got no response, he shouted his final question above the sound of the wind and waves.

"Is it my time, Rachel?"

He repeated it several times, sometimes imagining the answer had come back in the affirmative. After a while, he was filled with an inner peace and calmness in complete contrast to his surroundings. He no longer shouted his question and the noise of the wind and the sea became fainter and fainter. Though his head told him he was totally alone on the top of Canford Cliffs his heart told him he was not. He had finally reached his paradise and it was a far better place than the 'heaven on earth' he'd experienced for such a short time. He was with his beloved for eternity.

www.ingramcontent.com/pod-product-compliance
Ingram Content Group UK Ltd.
Pitfield, Milton Keynes, MK11 3LW, UK
UKHW041944190726
13854UKWH00004B/1791

9 781445 757551